Every day I Ball
BY MICHAEL SANDERS

They say I couldn't play football, I was too small.
They say I couldn't play basketball, I wasn't tall,
They say I couldn't bag chicks at all.
Now Every Day of My Life I Ball!

Everyday I Ball © 2010

ISBN: 978-0-615-40742-5

Published by: Justus Music Group/Seque Productions

This is a work of fiction. Names, characters, places, and incidents are either the product of the author's imagination or are used factiously. Any resemblance to actual persons, living or dead, or locales is entirely coincidental.

They say I couldn't play football, I was too small.
They say I couldn't play basketball, I wasn't tall,
They say I couldn't bag chicks at all.
Now Every Day of My Life I Ball!

**This book is dedicated in Loving memory of
Michaela Sacha Sanders
(Babygirl)**

*They say I couldn't play football, I was too small.
They say I couldn't play basketball, I wasn't tall,
They say I couldn't bag chicks at all.
Now Every Day of My Life I Ball!*

They say I couldn't play football, I was too small.
They say I couldn't play basketball, I wasn't tall,
They say I couldn't bag chicks at all.
Now Every Day of My Life I Ball!

TABLE OF CONTENTS

They say I couldn't play football, I was too small.
They say I couldn't play basketball, I wasn't tall,
They say I couldn't bag chicks at all.
Now Every Day of My Life I Ball!

Just the Beginning

All those late nights; the struggle is finally complete. I will like to thank a few people that was there for me in creating this masterpiece First and foremost I wanna thank God for making it possible and giving me the strength and guidance and focus, the most beautiful woman in the world letrice warren for all her smarts, ideas, and her New York swagg... My father thank you for always being there for me and never giving up on me and making me the man I am today. My mother for all her support and guidance and dicipline and believing in me. My brother thanks for being you and showed me a lot. Reggie Greene, thanks for giving me the idea from your football skills those days in North Carolina working out at nite. My protégé Anthony Ireland u going to make it, Trevor Graham, the best coach in the world. Joe Young Jr. good looking Joe always being there when I needed help and guiding me in the right directions. Special thanks to my editors, Sharon Arsego, Dan Banks, and graphic designer, Paul Szantyr aka Boogie, and Mary Dach. To my friend since Sacred Heart school Agron Belica for the final formatting of my manuscript. Lastly, my dude Razah this is just one of the steps to the top. Lastly, Tyler and Whirlee keep working you can achieve anything you want.

They say I couldn't play football, I was too small.
They say I couldn't play basketball, I wasn't tall,
They say I couldn't bag chicks at all.
Now Every Day of My Life I Ball!

About the Author

Michael Sanders is President and Founder of Seque Productions, a revolutionary film company providing a positive alternative that allows individuals the opportunity to build their self-confidence and self-esteem while becoming more well rounded, highly skilled individuals. Michael has enjoyed a successful ten year career as a professional international basketball player. Michael is also president of JustUs Music Group with R&B sensation and CEO Razah. 'Everyday, I Ball' is Michael's debut novel/feature film.

They say I couldn't play football, I was too small.
They say I couldn't play basketball, I wasn't tall,
They say I couldn't bag chicks at all.
Now Every Day of My Life I Ball!

"EVERY DAY I BALL"

PROLOGUE

It was just like any other day for these two 10yrs old best friends, they got together to partake in what could be considered their daily ritual; hop out of bed and head to the park to hang around on the monkey bars or just chill on the swings. However, the turn of events from this day will forever change their life.

The little league coach looked at the two kids standing on the sidelines hoping he would even the odds if one of them agreed to play. They had been there for quite some time watching the other kids playing football. Both looked like they could handle themselves on the field.

"Son, you wanna play?"

"Sure," the bigger of the two spoke up, "but I never played before, 'cept in the projects. So, I'm not very good.

"No matter, we only need one and that means you."

"Man, I'm gonna go watch the guys play some b-ball," the other one turned and headed across the street.

He stood behind the chain link fence and watched as one of the players drained a three to end the game.

"Hey kid, you wanna play?" asked one of the guys who had been waiting on the sidelines to get next.

The kid looked around and pointed at himself, "Who, me?"

"Yea, you lil' nigga. Come on."

They say I couldn't play football, I was too small.
They say I couldn't play basketball, I wasn't tall,
They say I couldn't bag chicks at all.
Now Every Day of My Life I Ball!

Hearing the screams from the football field, he chilled while his teammates hustled back to play some D. He looked over and saw his friend killing, juking, catching, and scoring touchdowns. The other little kids and even the coaches were cheering him on, watching in disbelief as the kid look like a pro whom had been playing all his life. "Damn, what the fuck?" one of them muttered to himself.

"Where did you get this kid?" the other one asked.

"He just walked up and I asked him if he wanted to play."

Back on the court like a carbon copy of what was happening on the football field; the other kid was crossing dudes and dropping dimes all over the court as if he were a little "skip to my lou" Rafer Alston.

"This kid is serious!" One of the players shook his head as he watched.

"How old are you?"

"Ten."

They say I couldn't play football, I was too small.
They say I couldn't play basketball, I wasn't tall,
They say I couldn't bag chicks at all.
Now Every Day of My Life I Ball!

In the Spotlight

"Thanks for tuning in, this is Sportcenter and I'm your host, Stewart Scott. Today's Sportcenter Spotlight is on Mizzier Sanders and Myshawn Greene, two huge names in the world of high school sports. Mizzier, better known as Mizzary or Mizz, and Myshawn, also known as Razah, for his sharp style and clean moves on the field, are both the number one ranked players in their respective high school sports. Mizzary's Sacred Heart High School's point guard, number one in his class academically and is president of the National Honor Society. Razah is Sacred Heart's running back, ranked second in his class and is vice-president of the National Honor Society. They are both fifteen year old sophomores and as you would think, they are the most popular tandem not only in their city and state, but in the nation.

These two kids have the whole package, including the game and the brains, and are both being heavily recruited by big-time universities. As sophomores, some analysts say they could both go pro right now and not only play, but be effective and do work. They haven't seen the likes of these student-athletes in these two sports in decades. In basketball, as the likes of Lebron James, Mizzary is America's new phenom. Razah on the other hand, has athleticism and lateral movement that we haven't seen since the acts of Walter Payton and Barry Sanders. He's like Michael Jackson with a football! Academically, they both have the ACT and SAT scores to qualify for college eligibility.

In their spare time, these two remarkable young men co-teach an ACT/SAT course. Some say Mizzier is a

They say I couldn't play football, I was too small.
They say I couldn't play basketball, I wasn't tall,
They say I couldn't bag chicks at all.
Now Every Day of My Life I Ball!

genius with an IQ of 168. Who else has an IQ of 168? Why none other than President Barack Obama. Folks, these two boys are a force to be reckoned with! The best part is, they are the best of friends and neighbors. Wow, what a great story! Folks, if that doesn't inspire you, get someone to check your pulse, because you're not breathing! This is Stewart Scott reporting from Sportscenter. Be easy."

They say I couldn't play football, I was too small.
They say I couldn't play basketball, I wasn't tall,
They say I couldn't bag chicks at all.
Now Every Day of My Life I Ball!

Business as Usual

Mizzier's alarm buzzed waking him to thoughts about what the new school year will bring. He stretched and rolled out of bed, kissed his chain, tapped his chest twice, looked up and said a little prayer; a ritual that he developed while in grade school and one that he has followed religiously since. Every good ball player has their little superstitions and this was his.

Surrounded by posters of Rafer Alston, Michael Jordan, and a few bikini models; clothes on the floor, shoes scattered and school books lying around, his room looked pretty typical for a fifteen year old and not what you would expect for a rising star genius athlete.

"Yo Mizz, you ready?"

"Yeah, be right down."

Today was the first day of school after a hot and crazy summer. Only sophomores, Mizz and Razah were possibly facing their last year of high school. Schools across the nation were eager to speak to them and rumors were even a few were willing to do what it took to get them to play college ball the next year. As they made their way, Mizz could see Razah wanted to share details about his adventures from last night.

"Yo sonn, what's good? That bitch was crazy last night kid." Razah said with a smile on his face.

"Yo, she suck you off ma' dude? You got your Jim Jones on?" Mizz wanted details.

"Hell yea nigga, she swallowed sonn."

"Ewhhh. She dumb nasty," Mizz said with a slight smirk. Changing the subject, he asked, "Anyways, how's

They say I couldn't play football, I was too small.
They say I couldn't play basketball, I wasn't tall,
They say I couldn't bag chicks at all.
Now Every Day of My Life I Ball!

your mom doin?"

"Sonn, same ol' same ol' you feel me?" Razah answered in a somber tone revealing just a little of the pain he was feeling inside.

As they continued on toward school, used crack bottles snapped under their feet while the daytime hoes stepped out from their dark corners to see if they could persuade the duo into a little three way for the right price.   Mizz and Razah crossed the street to avoid the shit and couldn't help but look back to take one last look at all the hood stars that had rolled out of bed nice and early to catch the school crowd.   After all, every dealer knows, if you get to them early, you got a customer for life. No matter how short that life was, they still pay to play. No strangers to the game, Mizz and Razah ran into their good friend Leak hustling on the corner.

"Yo Leak, what up dude? You stay getting money B. I wish I could get down wit that shit." Mizz said as he half hugged, half bumped Leak.

Following Mizz's lead, Razah spoke up. "Yea Leak, damn sonn. I saw that new whip you got. That shit hard. "

"You young niggas playin them sports and you niggas is mad smart. I saw you two clowns on Sportscenter last night. You two clowns really reppin' the hood, you feel me?"

"I feel you G. We tryin but we got no paper, no whip for the bitches. Nothin'."

"Nigga, we ain't got shit." Mizz and Razah rubbed their fingers together as if they were counting money.

"Well here you go, a lil' somethin'. It'll hold you down for a minute." Leak smiles knowing that staying on their good side may pay off for him some day.

> *They say I couldn't play football, I was too small.*
> *They say I couldn't play basketball, I wasn't tall,*
> *They say I couldn't bag chicks at all.*
> *Now Every Day of My Life I Ball!*

"Damn! Leak, good look. A "g" for both us. That's what's up."

"You niggas want a ride to school?"

"Nah, we good. Stay up Leak, holla back." Mizz and Razah turn to continue on to school.

"No doubt. Remember, M.O.B niggas. "

"No doubt."

Continuing on toward school they passed burned out cars and boarded-up abandoned buildings where apartments were used as "crack houses". A scene that these two have known their entire lives and were determined to make a distant memory.

Mizz breathed hard as the smell of urine and vomit filled his nostrils. "Sonn, we gotta get money kid. My mom just got laid off and my pops ain't doin' nothin' either. We just barely makin' ends meet. I gotta think of somethin'."

"Yo, I been thinkin' the same shit for the past month. Mizz, somethin' gotta give fo real." Razah said as he walked by a man laying face down in the gutter.

"Yo, we can get money from these niggas that's recruiting us, but you know the game kid. We gonna be obligated to these niggas. I'm not tryin' to send mixed signals."

"Yea sonn, you right. Even these niggas 'round our block, even Leak hit us off." Razah said.

"That's different, he fam." Mizz replied.

"True, true, whateva though."

"Yea, whateva."

As they approached the school, groups of kids gathered outside smoking and taking their last hits before the morning bell. Mizz and Razah learned to avoid the

They say I couldn't play football, I was too small.
They say I couldn't play basketball, I wasn't tall,
They say I couldn't bag chicks at all.
Now Every Day of My Life I Ball!

before school crowds and made their way towards a side entrance. After all, they had a rep they needed to maintain and they've learned the further they are from the everyday shit, the closer they got to reaching their goals.

As they passed a bulletin board with advanced classes offered for the school year, Mizz tapped the list and said, "Sonn, let's go see the guidance counselor and register for these classes. Since we both in the Honor Society, let's ask the nigga to give us college classes."

"Yo Mizz, I'm feelin' your "g" right now. Yo, probably out of these classes, somethin' will pop off to give us ideas on how to get this money kid."

"Razah, sonn. That's what I'm talkin' bout kid."

"That's why I fucks wit you." Razah said as he pushed Mizz ahead of him.

"Come on, let's change up this street mentality and let's get corporate. You know how we do."

"Yes sir." Razah says pretending to straighten a tie. With about fifteen minutes before their first class, they made their way to the guidance counselor's office. After the Sportscenter piece last night, Mizz and Razah were now looked at as true celebrities. Friends and teachers stopped them in the hall to share their thoughts, tell them congratulations and other meaningless shit that would hopefully keep them in their thoughts when then they went pro.

"Come in boys," Mr. Holmes called out from behind his desk as he spotted Mizz and Razah standing at his door. "Hey guys, how was your summer? I see that these colleges are really after you two, heavy. "

"Yes sir, they are most definitely trying to get our attention. " Mizz responded.

They say I couldn't play football, I was too small.
They say I couldn't play basketball, I wasn't tall,
They say I couldn't bag chicks at all.
Now Every Day of My Life I Ball!

"We need to stay focused and everything will fall into place." Myshawn said.

"Well, you fellas have the grades so it's all up to you. Anyway, what can I do for you two?"

"Well, Mr. Holmes, we want to take some college courses. We're up to the challenge." Mizzier said with confidence that was well beyond his fifteen years.

"We love making adjustments and this is a new endeavor we'd like to conquer." Myshawn said.

"Wow, you guys continue to impress me every day. No problem. Here is the list of classes. Just choose what's up your alley and we will take it from there. So go home guys, and get with me next week."

"We really appreciate you Mr. Holmes." They said as they smiled and left the office.

Five minutes now before their first class of their sophomore year, Mizz looked at Razah, "Sonn, we need to get on this kid."

"No doubt Mizz, I'll see you later. We will get up after school. I've got football practice, so meet me at my crib at eight."

"Holla back"

"No doubt." They bumped fists and headed their separate ways.

The day dragged for Razah as he thought about what Mizz and he talked about that morning. He needed money and so did Mizz, but how would they get it? He knew they could call in favors from the recruiters, but that could bite them in the ass later. They could hustle, but how much could that get them? Nah, it had to be something big and fast and he wasn't the thinker, Razah was sure that Mizz would come up with something. The last bell of the

They say I couldn't play football, I was too small.
They say I couldn't play basketball, I wasn't tall,
They say I couldn't bag chicks at all.
Now Every Day of My Life I Ball!

day rang and Razah headed for football practice.

At football practice, Coach Caine called Razah over for a little chat. "Razah, how was your summer? These colleges really on you heavy."

"Oh yea, like who, Coach? Enlighten me, Nah mean."

"Well, just to name a few conferences – the ACC, PAC 10, BIG 10, BIG 12, and BIG EAST. In those conferences, every team."

"So what you sayin'? I can go anywhere I want?"

"That's what I'm sayin' kid. Anywhere you want."

As Razah walked out of the locker room, he thought about the possibilities that were in front of him. Soon, those thoughts were replaced by images of hot cars, hoes and piles of cash. But all of that would have to wait at least three years, if not more depending on how his college career went. 'Nah,' he thought to himself,' ain't waiting that long.' 'Time to go see what Mizz is thinking.

Mizz looked at his clock. Just a little after eight and Razah should be there shortly.   He still couldn't believe how far the two of them had come and still had no paper to show for it.   Money was the goal and he had to figure out a way to get some. After looking at his school schedule and jotting down some ideas for he and Razah to go over, Mizz stood up and walked over to the window. He saw Razah at the door and motioned for him to come on up.

"Sonn, what's good?"

"Nigga, I got a plan my nigga fo real. I been checkin' out these classes for us kid.
If everything go accordin' to plan, we be paid nigga."

They say I couldn't play football, I was too small.
They say I couldn't play basketball, I wasn't tall,
They say I couldn't bag chicks at all.
Now Every Day of My Life I Ball!

"Sonn, you know I'm good wit everything. What's poppin'?" Razah had been waiting for this all day.

"Some of the research I been doin' is crazy ma nigga. But this is the shit. Well after talkin' to Mr. Holmes, he said we can get a jump on shit. So, here are the classes–Organic Chemistry, Bio-Chemistry, Pharmaceutics, Pharmacokinetics, Pharmacology, and Pharmaceutical Compounding." "What the fuck is that shit dude?"

"This is some high power shit sonn, feel me?"

"I can see kid, how did you come up wit this shit nigga?"

"Just readin' and shit. And remember the internship I did at the pharmacy, that summer? Pharmaceutical Compounding is how you make the drug into a tablet, a gel tablet."

"Drugs?"

"Yea kid, but this ain't heroine, crack cocaine, weed or the usual shit. This is some shit that's more addictive, completely legal and the way we gonna freak it is crazy. "

"Word, sonn?"

"Word. Sonn, we gonna make it into a piece of candy."

"Ewhhh!!! Say word." Razah nodded his head wanting to hear more.

"Word. Now we gotta figure how we gonna get the money for the machine in shit to make it. That's what's botherin' me."

"I got a plan sonn." Now it was Razah's turn to play.

"What kid?"

"I trust you, now you trust me."

They say I couldn't play football, I was too small.
They say I couldn't play basketball, I wasn't tall,
They say I couldn't bag chicks at all.
Now Every Day of My Life I Ball!

"No doubt, for life my nigga. Love always."
"Aight Mizz. I'm out. I'll have a plan in the next two days. True story."
"One."

They say I couldn't play football, I was too small.
They say I couldn't play basketball, I wasn't tall,
They say I couldn't bag chicks at all.
Now Every Day of My Life I Ball!

Razah's Reasons

The walk to school seemed a little bit different to Mizz as he and Razah discussed their future. They could smell the paper in the air as they headed into school and went straight to Mr. Holmes's office.

"Hey boys." Mr. Holmes greeted them.

"We have our classes." Mizz and Razah said with a just a slight cockiness in their voices.

"Okay, let me see what you have. Geez, wow, these classes are extremely hard. You guys ready for this?"

"Of course we are." They looked at each other and then back at Mr. Holmes.

"Alright, if it was anyone else, no way, but you guys can pull this off."

Mr. Holmes handed them the class schedules and shook their hands.

"Good luck, boys," he said as they turned and left his office, smiling and thinking about what lay ahead for them. School seemed to be the last thing on their minds as they anticipated the photo shoot with ESPN magazine that was set for them at the end of the day. At last the final bell rang and they were dismissed. They made their way to the gym first where the photographers had already set up their equipment and were waiting for the dynamic duo to arrive. They started with shots of him dropping dimes on his home turf. After about half an hour of lighting the gym up like a Christmas tree, they moved over to the football field to grab some frames of Razah in action. Another half hour passed and the camera crew moved the shoot to the front of the school where they took group shots of both Mizz and

They say I couldn't play football, I was too small.
They say I couldn't play basketball, I wasn't tall,
They say I couldn't bag chicks at all.
Now Every Day of My Life I Ball!

Razah together for the cover. When the shoot was over,
Mizz walked with Razah back to the football field where
practice had already started.

"Sonn, you come up wit the plan, kid?" Mizz
asked.

"Hell yea!" Razah responded enthusiastically.

"No doubt. We can talk later, word."

"Of course, I'll come over your crib after practice."
Razah said putting on his helmet. They bumped
fists and headed their separate ways. Later on that night,
Razah made his way to Mizz's crib. To his surprise, Mizz's
mom answered the door. Razah had been inside Mizz's
crib a million times before but tonight things looked a little
different. Not that they were different in a physical sense,
Razah's perspective was just different. The same old
checkered couches were in their same spot.   The same
stains were on the living room rug. The same light bulb
flickered in the corner lamp. And the same cream colored
paint was still peeling in the same places. But tonight, all
of these things began to feel like memories that Razah and
Mizz would soon be recalling as they sat sipping Cristal
and talking about what life used to be like. Razah's mind
jumped back to the present as Mizz's mom spoke.

"Hey boy, how are you doing? Long time."

"I been good. How's everything with you?"

"It's going." She said with a distressed look on her
face.

"I'll go get Mizz."

A few minutes later Mizz walked into the living
room and gestured toward the door.

"Sonn, what's good? Let's take a walk kid. I don't
wanna talk in the house."

They say I couldn't play football, I was too small.
They say I couldn't play basketball, I wasn't tall,
They say I couldn't bag chicks at all.
Now Every Day of My Life I Ball!

"I feel your "g", kid," Razah responded as he opened the front door and walking out into the still warm night air.

"So Sonn, holla at me. What you come up wit?" Mizz asked as they made their way down the street.

"Sonn, a heist."

"What, kid?!" Mizz wasn't sure he had heard his friend correctly.

"You heard me jigga boo, a heist!" Razah said sounding excited.

"Wow, kid! You a nut ass dude! How you expect to pull this off, nut ass nigga?"

"Have faith in me sonn, like I have faith in you kid."

"No doubt, I do. I just woulda never thought that we'd be talking 'bout this type of shit." Mizz said, shaking his head. He still couldn't believe what he had heard.

"I feel your "g", but son for real, how is it at on the home front, kid?" Razah said putting his hand on Mizz's shoulder.

"Sonn, it ain't good. Just barely makin' ends meet. You feel me? How 'bout you?"

"Same shit. Why you think I'm always comin' over your crib? This shit is bad, Mizz."

"One thing left to do. Let's get this money."

"No doubt. Holla back." Razah said as they dapped each other up and went their separate ways for the night.

The walk home from Mizz's house was short but Razah had already started to put together more details of his plan. They knew the right people in the right places to make it work. It had to work, because they needed money and they couldn't wait for their skills to pay the bills. No, they had to take matters into their own hands and make their own destiny.

They say I couldn't play football, I was too small.
They say I couldn't play basketball, I wasn't tall,
They say I couldn't bag chicks at all.
Now Every Day of My Life I Ball!

Neither one were able to sleep that night as they paced around their rooms each thinking about the next step to the plan.

"Damn!" Razah said to himself staring up at the ceiling as if calling on some extra help.

"Fuck!" Mizz said walking around still trying to get his head around what his friend had planned.

"I need to come with a plan of attack and a hardcore team of wolves, not goons, for this shit." Razah said as he climbed into bed.

"I need to get money. Now pops ain't workin', mom's be trippin'. Damn. I really need to get on my G, fuck." Mizz said to himself as he turned out his light for the night.

The next morning Razah sensed something weird about the house as he awoke. There was no noise, no sound, no yelling, nothing. He rolled out of bed and went to his little brother Mikey's room to find him still sleeping. Mikey had just turned seven and thought of Razah as his hero. He had pictures of his big brother from last year's championship game hanging over his bed. Razah looked at him, closed his door, and then went down the hall to his mother's room to find her bed was empty.

"What the fuck?" Razah thought to himself as he heard the sounds of his little brother waking up.

"Where's mommy?" Mikey stood there in his Sponge Bob pajamas looking to Razah for an answer, any answer.

"Not sure, lemme see if there's a note. Get ready for school, okay?"

"Okay." Mikey turned around and went back to his room.

Razah looked around the house and found no note,

They say I couldn't play football, I was too small.
They say I couldn't play basketball, I wasn't tall,
They say I couldn't bag chicks at all.
Now Every Day of My Life I Ball!

nothing to indicate where his mother had gone.

He went back to his brother's room. "I don't know where mommy is. I'm gonna get dressed and walk you to the bus stop."

Fifteen minutes later when they walked out the door, they found their mom standing on their front steps holding a bag of groceries. She was dressed in a short skirt and low-cut top with pumps, wearing lipstick and a leather jacket.

"Moms, where you been?" Razah said in an almost demanding tone.

"Grocery shopping," she said as if it was not out of the norm to look as she did for such a mundane chore. " Now don't ask me no more questions and take your brother to the bus," she snapped back.

Razah and Mikey walked in silence to the bus stop. Razah had his suspicions on where his Mom had been. As he watched Mikey get onto the bus, he hoped that he was wrong. Razah turned and started toward Mizz's house to see if they might be able to chat before they headed to school. He looked as tired as Razah felt.

"So I couldn't sleep at all last night kid." Mizz said still, half asleep.

"Me neither. Guess what though?"

"What kid?"

"My moms didn't come home last night. But this morning, she had mad groceries and pumps on." Razah said shaking his head trying to forget the scene from just a few minutes ago.

"Ewhhh! Cousin," Mizz said as if Razah had just slapped him in the face.

"Word." Replied Razah solemnly.

"Sonn, you think?"

They say I couldn't play football, I was too small.
They say I couldn't play basketball, I wasn't tall,
They say I couldn't bag chicks at all.
Now Every Day of My Life I Ball!

"I don't know kid, I don't know. But it don't look good and I know we need to get money."

"Sonn, for real dooke, for real," Mizz said following Razah's lead to change the subject. "What's really good?"

"I'm almost there kid. I was plottin' last night comin' up wit shit. Digg me?"

"Me too sonn. Real talk, me too."

"I was thinkin' of this shit." Razah rubbed his face thoughtfully. "We need wolves, not goons and straight family. I need to talk to Leak."

"Leak, he's our nigga. He will be down. He always feeding for action kid. Plus he real and I trust him." Mizz agreed. Razah heard Mizz but still had in his mind the image of his mom in pumps and that leather jacket. "Damn, life is crazy sonn," Razah said with a heavy sigh. "I got a game today. You goin' sonn?" he asked.

"Of course my nigga I'm goin'," Mizz said as if shocked that Razah even had to ask.

"I was wonderin' if my moms is goin'. If not, can you take Mikey for me?"

"Whateva sonn, anything."

"It's supposed to be on ESPN. Mad scouts suppose to be there. That's what coach said, but sonn I don't give a fuck. I'm on this paper chase."

"Sonn, I'll be there. We on the grind kid."

They arrived at school and headed to their separate classes. Neither of them could concentrate on any of the teacher's words that day. All they could think about was green. Even the upcoming game didn't keep Razah from working out the plan and how they were going to score. And Mizz just kept going over and over in his mind the

They say I couldn't play football, I was too small.
They say I couldn't play basketball, I wasn't tall,
They say I couldn't bag chicks at all.
Now Every Day of My Life I Ball!

formula that was going to make them stars.

Razah stretched and went through his pre-game ritual in the locker room. But, even with the biggest game of his life just minutes away, he couldn't shake the memory of his mom standing on the porch looking like, dam that was some bullshit this morning damn. He sat down on one of the benches, covered his face and tried to shift his focus back to the game when Coach Caine walked over to him and asked him to join him in the office.

"Are you ready? Just trying to give you a heads up. No pressure or anything, but this game is televised on ESPN and every major Division 1 scout will be checking out this game. I say this even though I know you have an unofficial visit to USC in couple days."

"Coach, I'm good. Pressure busts pipes and I'm a wolf. Anyways, I got other things on my mind. This game, truth be told, is the least of my worries."

"What do you mean?" Coach asked cautiously, trying not to reveal the worry that he was starting to feel.

"Ah, Coach," Razah said with a half hearted reassuring grin, "this is what I was born to do. This game is minor to me. Looks like you stressin' more than me."

"I'm just making sure you're ready brother," Coach Caine said touching Razah's shoulder.

"I'm good. Thanks." Razah turned and walked toward the tunnel that led out to the field where thousands of people were waiting to see the much talked about sensation, who at the moment, could care less.

With just seconds before the kickoff, Razah stood on the field and looked around trying to locate his mom, Mikey, or Mizz. Mizz saw him and stretched his arms out to get Razah's attention. Razah smiled as Mizz bumped his

They say I couldn't play football, I was too small.
They say I couldn't play basketball, I wasn't tall,
They say I couldn't bag chicks at all.
Now Every Day of My Life I Ball!

chest twice to let him know that it was game time. Razah
did the same and saluted his little brother who was standing
next to Mizz. Mikey returned the salute just as the kickoff
came. The ball sailed through the air all the way back to
the one yard line, where Razah caught it and took off like a
rocket.

"Yo, run sonn, run!" Mizz shouted as Razah spun
and dodged tackle after tackle and ran back the opening
kickoff for a touchdown. Razah stood in the end zone
looking at his little brother who was holding up a sign that
read, "It's Time to Be Ill". In that moment, that one brief
moment, Razah forgot about the morning, the paper, the
hood, he forgot about everything, and played like he was
born to. At the end of the game, the stats said it all. He had
rushed for over 250 yards and four touchdowns and had led
his team to victory. The ESPN analysts went crazy. The
crowd couldn't stop cheering and Razah's coaches stood
speechless, in awe of the performance they had just
witnessed. Coach Caine walked out onto the field and put
his arm around Razah.

"I should never have underestimated you. Damn!
Your game was great tonight. Schools were going crazy. I
know my phone will be ringing off the hook this week."

"Thanks coach." Razah said in a somewhat somber
tone.

"You don't seem happy at all. You wanna talk about
it? You had a great game kid. What seems to be the
problem?"

"Nothin' coach, I'm good."

"You sure?"

"Of course, coach I'm chillin'," Razah said as he
turned and walked out of the locker room to face the

They say I couldn't play football, I was too small.
They say I couldn't play basketball, I wasn't tall,
They say I couldn't bag chicks at all.
Now Every Day of My Life I Ball!

reporters who were waiting to interview the high school phenomenon. All the lights, all the cameras, all the hype couldn't drag Razah's mind away from the plan that had begun to take even more shape while he played the game of his life. After the interviews, he was exhausted and was happy to have Mizz and Mikey waiting for him.

"Damn sonn, Razah!!! You was givin' it to them niggas," Mizz said bumping chests with Razah.

"Yea brother, they couldn't see you," Mikey said expressing some of the pride he was feeling being a super star's brother.

"Moms ain't come huh?" Razah asked already knowing the answer.

"Nah, she had to work late," Mikey said, knowing how that hurt his big brother.

"Oh well, fuck it." Razah sighed and then straightened up a little.

"It's all good sonn. She'll be at the next one." Mizz said hoping to ease a little of his friend's pain.
"Sonn, except for a few times, the whole game, all I thought about was getting' money ma' nigg."

"Damn nut ass nigga. You wasn't focused?" Mizz asked in shock.

"Psh, focused on that money. I play great ball in my sleep. Shit, I was lookin' in the stands, saw all them hoes. I was ready to get my Jigga and Diddy on, but I remember I ain't got no paper." Razah rubbed his fingers together.

"Damn you a fool. I would hate to see you when you focused 'cause ma' dude it was ugly sonn. I was like, Razah he dumb nasty."

"Thanks cuzo, but I need this paper.""Did you

They say I couldn't play football, I was too small.
They say I couldn't play basketball, I wasn't tall,
They say I couldn't bag chicks at all.
Now Every Day of My Life I Ball!

come up wit the rest of the plan yet?" Mizz asked.

"Jus' have a few more glitches to fix kid." Razah stopped and looked at Mizz. "It gotta be perfection, ya dig? I'm tryin' to be like Marlo on 'The Wire'."

"Hmm. That nigga hard." Mizz agreed.

"That shit wit my moms is trippin' me out." Mizz placed a reassuring hand on his friend's shoulder, "Sonn, it's nothin', stop buggin'."

"You right sonn, it's just my moms. Feel me?" Razah said, sounding a little annoyed.

"No doubt bro, I feel your pain. But sonn, stay focused on what we doin' B." replied Mizz trying to smooth over the moment.

"Fo sho." Replied Razah as they reached his house. Realizing the time, Mizz started his goodbye. "Sonn, holla back kid. Great game." Mizz bumped fists with Razah and headed toward home.

"No doubt B. Mikey, you can tell Mizz later." Razah said.

"Later Mizz." Mikey waved as Mizz crossed the street.

"We will get up tomorrow." Razah called over.

"Cool." Mizz said.

Once they got home, Razah and Mikey opened the door only to find all the lights off and seemingly no one at home. "Mom, you home?" Razah called into the darkness. No answer. Razah felt a little sick to his stomach thinking about where she might be. Not wanting to give Mikey any cause to worry and figuring he might be hungry, he suggested that they go up the block and grab some pizza. On their way, they saw a black Porsche Cayenne Turbo with black tints parked on the corner.

They say I couldn't play football, I was too small.
They say I couldn't play basketball, I wasn't tall,
They say I couldn't bag chicks at all.
Now Every Day of My Life I Ball!

"Mikey, that car is hot," Razah said thinking again about how to get some paper.

"I like it," Mikey replied.

"I will get one of these, watch."

As they walked into the pizza shop, the owner of the car stepped out and started talking to them. He was dressed in a black leather trench coat that went all the way down to his brown crocodile leather shoes. On his fingers were big diamond rings and around his neck were even bigger gold chains. He smiled at Razah, revealing his abnormally white teeth.

"Hey kid, ain't you that superstar running back dude? Damn, you nice."

"Not like this whip. Damn, what you do man?" Razah asked looking at the car.

"I own my own business. One of my employees is comin' out right now. I'll let you meet her. Then you can find out what I do, kid."

"Cool, no doubt." Razah said as the door to the pizza shop opened behind them.

"Hey babe, meet the next Barry Sanders." The man said as Razah and Mikey turned around.

"Mom, what's good? What are you doin'?" Razah asked almost stuttering.

"Mom? What the fuck? This your son? What, you got a son?" The man said almost stuttering himself.

"Mom, what are you doin'?" Razah asked again, this time shaking a little bit. "Are you serious?"

"What are you and Mikey doin' outside at this hour?" His mom replied dodging the questions. "We just came from my game and Mikey was hungry."

They say I couldn't play football, I was too small.
They say I couldn't play basketball, I wasn't tall,
They say I couldn't bag chicks at all.
Now Every Day of My Life I Ball!

"Two kids?! This shit is crazy. I'm out." The man started to get back into his car.

"Wait, Anton, wait for me, I'm still going with you," Razah's mom said to her boss. To Razah she glared and said. "Razah, I will see you at home."

"What's good? You straight?" The man looked at Razah and then at her.

She nodded her head turning her eyes away from her boys. The man took her hand and opened the car door for her. She got in and they drove off.

"Damn, I wonder what was mom doin' wit that nigga." Razah said out loud not really asking anyone. "Fuck, this is it. I'm gonna get this money. This bullshit is enough." Razah said clenching his teeth and narrowing his eyes. They walked into the pizza shop and ordered a pepperoni to go. Both of them stood in silence as they waited for their pizza.

Sitting at home later and with Mikey sleeping soundly, Razah's mom finally walked in the door. She turned toward Razah and spoke.

"Son, come here please."

"Yes mom?"

"What do you think I was doin' with that guy?"

"Honestly ma, I don't wanna know." Razah said hoping the conversation would go no further.

"All right son."

"Mom, I did well tonight at the game. I'm tired mom." Razah got up and walked toward the stairs. "See you in the morning. Goodnight, I love you ma."

"All right son. Goodnight baby, I love you."

As Razah walked up the stairs, he didn't see his mom sit down on the couch and put her face into her hands. He

They say I couldn't play football, I was too small.
They say I couldn't play basketball, I wasn't tall,
They say I couldn't bag chicks at all.
Now Every Day of My Life I Ball!

didn't hear her start to cry. She didn't see him sit on his bed and put his face into his hands. Nor did she hear him start to cry. He needed that paper, not just for the hoes, not just for the cars, not just for the shit, no he needed that paper to survive. He closed his eyes and went to sleep.

They say I couldn't play football, I was too small.
They say I couldn't play basketball, I wasn't tall,
They say I couldn't bag chicks at all.
Now Every Day of My Life I Ball!

The Wiz

Razah couldn't sleep again that night. He kept thinking about his mom, that dude, Anton, the plan, and what he had to do to get away from all of this shit. He got out of his bed and looked up to the ceiling as if praying to get the answer he needed. Then it hit him, exactly what needed to be done to pull the heist off without any problems. He tapped his chest twice, saluted toward the ceiling as if thanking whoever might be on the other side and went back to bed.

The next morning, he got dressed in a hurry and practically ran out the door so he didn't have to see or talk to his mom. Moments later, he stood outside of Mizz's house and knocked. Mizz looked out his window and told Razah to come on up.

"Sonn, guess what?" Razah said as he met Mizz in the hall.

"What's good ma dude?" Questioned Mizz.

"Saw ma dukes wit this nigga last night in a Porsche truck."

"Say word. Black on black my nig?"

"Yeah."

"Ewwwh sonn," Mizz shook his head. "What happened cuzin?"

"When moms came home, I was like 'I don't wanna know nothin' kid.' But I do know we gotta get this money."

"We will, we will.

"Few more days, we should be straight. Just a few more days my nig."

"Yo B, we got that meeting today."

They say I couldn't play football, I was too small.
They say I couldn't play basketball, I wasn't tall,
They say I couldn't bag chicks at all.
Now Every Day of My Life I Ball!

"What meeting?" Razah asked, having completely forgotten.

"With the National Honor Society."

"Oh yea, Mr. President," Razah laughed.

"That's right Mr. Vice President, my nigga," said Mizz gettin' all presidential. "I'm like Obama out this bitch. You feel me?" They laughed and headed to school.

Later on that day after being introduced by the secretary as vice president and president, Myshawn and Mizzier addressed the group.

"How was everyone's summer? For those that don't know, I'm Myshawn, vice president and I'm happy to meet all of you. Let's continue to strive in our daily endeavors. I'm not one for long speeches, so I'll be brief and turn it over to the President, Mizzier." Razah turned and gestured toward Mizz.

"Thank you, Vice President Myshawn, for that introduction. Good afternoon. It's a pleasure to see old and new faces alike. Let's get down to business, shall we? First notion, let's give respect to all those that have left us and achieved great new endeavors in college, and let us follow in their footsteps and positive influence. Hard work and a clean slate will get us to where we have to go and we will still rise." Mizz stood straight as the audience rose to their feet and clapped indicating their agreement with his words. He turned, looked at Razah and smiled.

Later on that day, Razah caught up with Mizz and pulled him aside. "Yo sonn, we need to talk."

"Word." Mizz shook his head in agreement.

"Word."

"That's what I'm talking 'bout cuz. Cool."

"Sonn, I will come to your crib after football

They say I couldn't play football, I was too small.
They say I couldn't play basketball, I wasn't tall,
They say I couldn't bag chicks at all.
Now Every Day of My Life I Ball!

practice."

"No doubt." They dap each other up and Razah heads off to get ready for practice.

A little while later, Razah sat in the locker room after practice when Coach Caine walked up and addressed his star player. "Hey Razah, you ready for this week? You have an unofficial visit to USC. What do you think?"

"I always liked USC, especially when Reggie Bush was there. He was my dude."

"I think this is smart," Coach continued, "you going on an unofficial visit out there."

"I have family there and I lucked up cuz the school's flying me out there for the National Honor Society conference. So I figure, why not kill two birds with one stone, right? Go there unofficially so I don't waste one of my five visits," Razah said tapping his head as if indicating his intelligence.

"You gotta be the luckiest and blessed kid I know."

"Thanks coach," responded Razah as he stood up, walked out of the locker room, and headed straight for Mizz's crib.

Twenty minutes later, Razah knocked on the door and waited for Mizz. Mizz opened it and motioned for Razah to come in. "Hold up a sec, while I grab my coat.

"Let's go to the pizza spot and talk kid." Razah said as they walked out the door.

"Cool, I'm hungry anyway." They headed across the street and up the block to their favorite pizza joint.

They walked into the shop and ran into their friend Marty, the pizza shop owner. "Hey guys, if it ain't the world's two best athletes." Marty said smiling.

"Marty, what's good bro? How's everything?"

They say I couldn't play football, I was too small.
They say I couldn't play basketball, I wasn't tall,
They say I couldn't bag chicks at all.
Now Every Day of My Life I Ball!

Mizz replied.

"You guys got the good life. I'm just tryin' to live."

"Yea right, you straight." Mizz said.

"You do mad business." Razah added. "You always packed."

"Thanks.   What can I get you guys?   It's on the house. It's always on the house for you two.

"We got you when we get on." Razah promised.

"I know brothers, I know." Marty said shaking his head. "Now, what you guys want?"

"The usual," they said.

"All right guys, be good." Marty said as he headed back into the kitchen.

"That nigga be holdin' us down." Razah said as they sat down in an empty booth.

"No doubt cuzo, what's good tho' nigga?" Mizz wanted to get down to business.

"You know we got that Honor Society school shit meeting next week in Cali." Razah started, "And I'm visiting USC too."

"Ok and what?" Mizz inquired.

"Well, I've been talkin' to my cousin. Remember he came out here last week?   So, I was tellin' him about my idea and he said he'd be down for whateva.   My other cousin put me down wit this dude wit plans for the bank and everything.   I gotta meet him tomorrow.   Here's the shit. The bank is in Cali and it's the perfect alibi.   Why not take it down while we out there sonn?"

"Bank cuzin?" Mizz said in disbelief. "You done bumped your motherfuckin' head!"

"Yo sonn, trust me for real.   On doggz," Razah said tapping his chest.

They say I couldn't play football, I was too small.
They say I couldn't play basketball, I wasn't tall,
They say I couldn't bag chicks at all.
Now Every Day of My Life I Ball!

"On doggz? Damn sonn, you must be for real cuz that sayin' is madd old." Mizz said half laughing.

"Man listen," Razah said just a little too loud. "Trust me."

"I feel you. Your cousins, them niggas wolves?"

"Most definitely, this is our chance. I will find out the score when I meet dude tomorrow. You know how to handle a Mac 10?"

"Nah, but hopefully we ain't gotta use it." Mizz now saw that Razah was serious about this. "Sonn, you real wit this?" "No doubt. My plan is to a T. One shot. It's like a buzzer beater and a game winning touchdown. We will own this fuckin' city," Razah said looking straight into Mizz's eyes as Marty brought out their order.

That night, Razah still could not sleep. His mind buzzed with anticipation of what was about to happen. He felt it in his blood. The next day he would meet up with his cousin and the man that would help put his plan into action. After that, there was no stopping them. He closed his eyes and let himself think about what life would be like with real paper in their pockets. With visions of hot honeys in short skirts and crazy expensive cars, Razah finally fell asleep.

The next day Razah met up with his cousin, Cuzo, outside an old office complex. The building was abandoned with boarded up windows and no trespassing signs posted throughout. Cars with their insides gutted and burned out covered the landscape making this a perfect place to meet in privacy since no one in their right mind would make the mistake of walking back there. Razah and Cuzo gave each other a quick hug and then got right down to business.

"Razah, this is my man, a real old G. They call him Wiz." Cuzo gestured toward the man standing at the

They say I couldn't play football, I was too small.
They say I couldn't play basketball, I wasn't tall,
They say I couldn't bag chicks at all.
Now Every Day of My Life I Ball!

building's entrance. The man stood about six feet tall and looked to be in his fifties. Dressed in a black suit with a black shirt, and black shoes with a diamond stud in both ears, his mere presence demanded respect. "We used to think he worked at the parliament, all this money he used to get."

"Hey young blood," Wiz spoke shaking Razah's hand. "Your cousin told me so much about you. So why you wanna deal wit the inner thieves?"

"Well its simple arithmetic," Razah began. "I can continue to prosper and struggle or I can continue to prosper and get money too. I prefer havin' the best of both worlds, feel me?"

"Ok young blood. I feel your gangsta. Step into my office." The wizard opened the door and motioned for Razah to step inside.

"Ok, I got everything nailed to a T, so if you fuck up, you're a dickhead. And you snitch on anybody, you're a dead man," Wiz said with a shrug. " But you already know that, so there's no need to emphasize it. Capeesh?" Wiz's face changed to reveal the hard interior that existed under the soft designer fabric of his suit.

"Capeesh," Razah quickly replied.

"Ok, now bizness ma nigga. Here's the deal. We'll hit at the end of the week," the wizard said as he began to layout the plan.

"Thursday?" Razah asked

"Of course. You're sharp kid. That's when they get chips and give the paper to all the other banks in the area. So their asses are good for check day, which is Friday, and payroll, of course. So the head bank of the area got all the paper," He continued.

They say I couldn't play football, I was too small.
They say I couldn't play basketball, I wasn't tall,
They say I couldn't bag chicks at all.
Now Every Day of My Life I Ball!

"How many mothafuckas?" Razah interrupted.

"Three or four. Bust 'em bastards and you out clear as day," Wizard smiled.

"So Wiz, you want 150 stacks just for that?" Razah's tone changed. "That shit ma dude and 10% of the earnings? Damn, Wiz. Man listen, you bumped your mothafuckin' head. Fuck, them mothafuckas gonna hit up the holdup alarm. I gotta bounce before the pigs come. What the fuck is that Wiz?"

"Nephew, they hit up three hold up joints. Young blood, in case you don't know Spanish, two telecoms plus a cellular."

"Word," Razah shook his head starting to understand.

"Yea, check it out though. The signals ain't goin' a mothafuckin' place cuz the night before, you and your crew cut in and trigger out the alarm system PC to program the shit to turn the video cameras and recorders off 30 minutes before you do your thing, feel me?" Wiz sat down in a nice leather office chair behind a solid oak desk as he continued to speak.

"Hell yea I feel you nigga," Razah replied.

"Here are the architectural, electrical, and engineering plans. My lil' nigga, I got all the semantics, the boards and shit already built to the PC."

"Damn, dude. You got all that shit. What's the take, Wiz?"

"10.1, 10.2 million."

"No doubt old school, you on!" Razah's eyes almost popped out of his head.

"That's the estimate sonn. I got a print out if you wanna check it out though."

"Ewhh!!! Word."

They say I couldn't play football, I was too small.
They say I couldn't play basketball, I wasn't tall,
They say I couldn't bag chicks at all.
Now Every Day of My Life I Ball!

"Why you think they call me Wiz? But congrats, young blood. Again I got everything or access to it."

"I see, I see. Thanks, we'll be in touch," Razah turned and started towards the door.

"I know you will, I know you will," Wiz spoke almost under his breath as he watched Razah and Cuzo leave. Cuzo pulled up the whip and Razah got in.

They say I couldn't play football, I was too small.
They say I couldn't play basketball, I wasn't tall,
They say I couldn't bag chicks at all.
Now Every Day of My Life I Ball!

Time is Money

Razah met up with Mizz and told him about the plan.

"Sonn, we good. Look at all that shit," Razah said showing Mizz the plans that Wiz had given him.

Mizz looked at them. "Damn, you could build a bank wit this shit."

Later, Razah sat down in his room with the paper work that Wiz gave him and went over the plot step by step. He felt like something was missing. He knew there had to be something else to make sure that this would look like an inside job. He needed a way to speak with his crew without it being traced. 'A boost prepaid would work,' he thought to himself, and he headed out to find one.

After picking up the phone at a local store, he went in search for a payphone. He found one outside a gas station. Looking around to make sure no one could hear him; he picked up the phone and called the crew. He gave them the password that Wiz had given him and laid out the plans for them using pig Latin to throw off any would-be listeners.

Three hours later, Razah holla'd back at his peeps and went over the math once again with them. This time he called from a different pay phone. Then using the prepaid, he shot Wiz a text asking for a list of all the security guards on duty in the bank, their addresses, and their phone numbers. Wiz texted him back that it wasn't a problem and to give him an hour.

An hour later Wiz gave Razah the information. Razah dumped the prepaid in a nearby alley and dumped the battery in the sewer and pockets the sim card. Razah went back to his crib and looked up on the internet what security company the bank used. From there, he found out where

They say I couldn't play football, I was too small.
They say I couldn't play basketball, I wasn't tall,
They say I couldn't bag chicks at all.
Now Every Day of My Life I Ball!

they were located and what kinds of uniforms they wear. He then called the security guards that would be on duty the day of the heist and told them there was a last minute convention and that they will get paid time and a half, plus overtime pay and mileage for coming. They all agreed.

The headquarters where the convention was taking place was hours away from the bank. The convention was at one, the same time his crew was set to bust down the bank. In the meantime, Razah's cousin's homie worked at the spot where the company gets their uniforms made so they were straight with the look of authority they needed to place them in the bank.

During an earlier trip to the site, Mizz and Razah had scoped out the bank from garage. Razah borrowed his uncle's truck to do the electrical work on the PC from the underground. Looking at the plans they found the perfect spot to drill through the floor of the bank from the garage.

They drilled through for a potential coming in and exiting point. After setting up a ladder for a quick getaway, they went back to the crib.

Before the heist, Razah got everyone down. "Okay fellas, here it is." Razah began. "I need to know who's in right now. Fuck everything you said before, this is our problem. Take the bank or split right now. Mizz?" Razah looked at his best friend already knowing the answer.

Mizz bumped his chest twice as he answered. "You know I'm in of course. Ride or die."

"Nice to see you made it out here, Cuzo. You in?" Razah asked his cousin

"Hell yea." Cuzo enthusiastically replied.

"Nico?" Razah continued.

"Fuck yea my nigga." Nico said with conviction.

They say I couldn't play football, I was too small.
They say I couldn't play basketball, I wasn't tall,
They say I couldn't bag chicks at all.
Now Every Day of My Life I Ball!

"Cool. We got work to do." Razah raised his hands in invitation to his friends to join him. They gathered around him like he was their coach and pledged their loyalty to the task at hand.

They say I couldn't play football, I was too small.
They say I couldn't play basketball, I wasn't tall,
They say I couldn't bag chicks at all.
Now Every Day of My Life I Ball!

The Heist

Cuzo stood in his room admiring how he looked in the security officer uniform. He wondered if he would have a better chance of scoring with the ladies if he showed up dressed like that. He laughs, realizing he was wearing what was essentially a toy soldier's uniform. He straightened his tie, put on his plastic badge, and left.

Only a few blocks away, Nico, was just about to leave when the sweet little thing he picked up at the club the night before pulled him back inside. She ran her hands up and down his sky blue shirt and tugged at his tie. "I don't know what it is boy, but this uniform is making me all wet. I wish you didn't have to go to work," she purred sweetly. He looked at her thinking if only she knew what he was actually going to be doing, and flashed a crooked smile. Not that he would keep her around long enough to share anything with her anyway. Wearing nothing but one of his shirts, she stood there tempting him to stay just a little bit longer. He thought about it a second, but then green and nothing but green filled his mind. Pussy was one thing, but paper was quite another and he was not going to blow his chance at the kind of paper he stood to gain with the heist. He kissed her one last time, told her to lock the door on her way out, and left. A few hours later, posted inside the bank, Nico and Cuzo stood at the front door and looked at their watches. In just five minutes, all hell would break loose. Under the bank's floor, Razah and Mizz waited patiently for the signal.

Five minutes later, Nico stepped outside and lit a cigarette, giving the signal to the rest of the crew who were waiting in the garage across the street. Razah and Mizz put

They say I couldn't play football, I was too small.
They say I couldn't play basketball, I wasn't tall,
They say I couldn't bag chicks at all.
Now Every Day of My Life I Ball!

their ear pieces in, pulled stocking caps over their faces, and switched the safeties off on the Mac 9's. The lights in the bank went out and immediately the people inside started screaming. Razah set the timer on his watch to go off in five minutes.

"This is it," Mizz looked at Razah. "Ride or die."

"Hell, yeah. Let's do it my nigga." They dapped each other up then Razah pulled two smoke grenades out of his pack and lifted the loosened floor tile just enough to roll them along the floor. As they exploded, Mizz and Razah pushed through the floor tile, climbed into the bank and moved into position.

"Everyone get up against the wall. We want the bank's money, not yours. Your money is insured by the federal government," Mizz said trying to calm the situation down. "You can thank your lovely President Barack Obama for that."

"We don't wanna hurt anyone. Please don't try to be a hero. You will get fucked up, please believe. Now everyone put your hands where I can see them and get on the wall." Razah waved his gun in the air motioning for everyone to move.

Cuzo and Nico raised their hands up and made their way over to the wall as if they had no idea what was going on. Razah walked over to the bank supervisor, looked at his name tag that read 'Jerry', and asked him for the key to the vault. The supervisor looked at Razah as if he had no idea where it was.

"What key?" He asked in a shaky voice. This was Jerry's thirty fifth year with only a few months left until retirement. He wasn't going to let some punks get away with the first heist in the bank's history.

They say I couldn't play football, I was too small.
They say I couldn't play basketball, I wasn't tall,
They say I couldn't bag chicks at all.
Now Every Day of My Life I Ball!

"I said, don't fuck with me. Now where is the fuckin' key?" Razah asked again lifting his gun. And without waiting for an answer, he cracked Jerry square in the face snatching the key from around his neck. Blood spurted from the supervisor's nose as he fell to the floor with his head in his hands. "How do you like that, Jerry?" Razah asked, almost smiling. He then handed the key to Mizz to open the vault. Mizz grabbed three black duffle bags out of his backpack, walked into the vault, and began filling them up with cash. Looking at his watch to check their progress, he filled each bag and slid them across the floor to Razah.

"Everybody keep your head down, head down!" Razah yelled at the group of people standing against the wall, most either crying or praying when Razah's watch timer went off.

"We gotta bounce." Razah said into his microphone.

"We straight! We straight!" Mizz called out.

Mizz pulled out two more smoke grenades and rolled them across the floor. They exploded and then the lights went off, as Razah, Mizz, Cuzo, and Nico dropped through the floor, with no indication that they were ever there. They made their way through the sewer and across the street to the garage where they met up with the rest of their crew then continued through the sewer until they reached the alley where Razah had dumped the phone earlier. They climbed out of the sewer and looked around. Everything seemed cool.

"Fuck, I feel like a rat. That sewer was dumb nasty," Nico said as he brushed off dust from his uniform.

"Yeah, but we mother fuckin' rich rats," Mizz said tapping the duffel bag he was holding.

They say I couldn't play football, I was too small.
They say I couldn't play basketball, I wasn't tall,
They say I couldn't bag chicks at all.
Now Every Day of My Life I Ball!

"And if we get caught, we'll be dead fuckin' rats," Razah interrupted, "Now let's go!" They exited the alley and headed over to a black Escalade that Nico had obtained from the parking lot at the club the night before.

"Damn, nothing like riding in style," Cuzo said.

"Get used to it, because this is just the beginning," Mizz said as he began throwing the duffel bags into the back seat.

They changed clothes in the car then drove a short distance to Razah's uncle's truck. Razah and Mizz got into the truck and watched as Nico and Cuzo threw gasoline all over the stolen car and ignited it. Just as Nico and Cuzo climbed into the truck, the Escalade exploded taking with it all evidence of the heist. Mizz shifted the truck into drive and sped off down the city streets on the escape route they had mapped out.

Razah looked at Mizz, "Sonn, that shit was hard kid, but when we leave this car, let's not mention it again."

"My nigga, my adrenaline was crazy," Mizz said. "That shit was to a T."

"Razah!!! Razah!!! Cousin." Cuzo said shaking Razah's shoulders.

"Word sonn, word." Nico added.

They soon reached their Uncle's crib, a small house located at the end of a dead-end street in an even more dead-end neighborhood. If you weren't from this area or weren't with someone form this area, your chances of survival were pretty thin. Mizz and Razah lived in a pretty rough area back in New York, but this was Compton and they knew its reputation well, not only from Cuzo's stories but also from news that they had seen or read many times. Everyone knew, you don't fuck around in Compton. They got out of

They say I couldn't play football, I was too small.
They say I couldn't play basketball, I wasn't tall,
They say I couldn't bag chicks at all.
Now Every Day of My Life I Ball!

the truck and hustled the bags into the house.

"Yo, I'm about to go on my unofficial visit to USC. Uncle is gonna take me over there. In the meantime, you niggas get the money machine and count that shit," Razah motioned toward the basement.

"No doubt, kid. I got you," Mizz said. "But Razah, how we gonna take this paper with us?"

"When you niggas go in the basement, there are two big ass plastic bins filled with Styrofoam and books. My cousin, Casey is a manager at Fed Ex. In the morning, we'll bring it to her crib and she'll overnight it to this old folk's home where Leak's girl works at. When it arrives, Leak will pick it up."

"Damn, so you go this shit to a T my nigga. Aight sonn, we good. We gonna handle that, holla back. And remember, yo sonn, don't sign," Mizz said referring to the USC visit and punching Razah in the shoulder.

"Good look, hell no. We goin' to the same school." Razah reassured Mizz.

"No doubt, 100."

"100."

They say I couldn't play football, I was too small.
They say I couldn't play basketball, I wasn't tall,
They say I couldn't bag chicks at all.
Now Every Day of My Life I Ball!

USC

Razah's uncle came over and let Razah know he was ready to go. Razah grabbed his coat and headed out. When he arrived at the school there was a parade waiting for him. He felt like royalty as he climbed out of his uncle's ride and saw students with signs and shirts, even printed jerseys with his name on it. The coach walked up and put his arm around him.

"You are the best running back I've ever seen. You're ready for the NFL right now. I can see why they call you Razah, Mr. Sharp Dresser." Razah had made sure to look sharp to make a good impression even though he knew he wasn't gonna sign that day while the coach seemed to be more of a fan than a guy set on recruiting him.
Razah chuckled to himself. "Thanks for the compliments, Coach. Ready for the NFL? You really feel that way?"

"Absolutely. Uncle, you gotta be proud of Myshawn. By the way, where's your sidekick Mizzier?"

"He's hanging back ready for the school conference in the morning."

"That's good. I never heard of a tandem like you two before. Hopefully both of you will consider us and attend school together here." The coach said this time patting Razah on the back.

"Coach I really appreciate that, especially all these kind words coming from a person of your caliber and success."

"Well, what we have in store for you today is a football game so you can see how we work. Let me bring you both to the locker room to meet the guys."

"Wow, I would love that," Razah said as they headed

They say I couldn't play football, I was too small.
They say I couldn't play basketball, I wasn't tall,
They say I couldn't bag chicks at all.
Now Every Day of My Life I Ball!

toward the locker room.

The coach introduced him and his uncle to all of the players who were suiting up for the game. They also acted more like his fans than potential team mates. The coach then led Razah to his own locker where a jersey with his name on it was hanging inside.

"This is unbelievable. I can't believe this." Razah said picking up the jersey.

"So what do you think?"

"This is a dream. I don't wanna wake up."

"Ok," said the coach as he smiled to himself, "I'm going to give the pre-game talk and get them ready." The coach moved to the center of the locker room. "Please listen in."

Coach talked to his team and got them all hyped up. They were ready to do work. Coach brought Razah aside and told him to walk out with them onto the field. Playing on the big screen were highlights of Razah making fools out of his opponents. The crowd chanted, 'We want Razah! We want Razah!' Razah stood there mesmerized.

'So this is what the fuss is all about,' he said to himself.

"You deserve this Myshawn, you deserve this." His uncle walked over to him and put his arm around him.

The coach called them over and asked if they wanted to join the team on the sidelines for the game. He couldn't believe the stops they were pulling out for him. He and his uncle watched from the best spot in arena as USC trounced their rivals UCLA. It was a great experience for the both of them. After the game, the coach called them back into the locker room.

"So what you think? This something here you

They say I couldn't play football, I was too small.
They say I couldn't play basketball, I wasn't tall,
They say I couldn't bag chicks at all.
Now Every Day of My Life I Ball!

wanna come to?" He asked making no attempt at hiding his excitement.

"Of course. You're in my top 5." Razah replied.

"Wow, you can sign right now, if you want to." The coach pulled a pen out of his pocket.

"I'm not ready, but we will be in touch."

"I can respect that Myshawn".

"Thanks."

"Do you need anything? Anything?" The coach asked with a hint of promise in his voice.

"I'm good. We are going to go. I have that conference tomorrow." Razah said.

"Good luck and stay in touch."

"Of course we will. Coach, thanks for having me."

"Anytime. Remember, anything you need, anything at all, just pick up the phone."

Razah and his uncle left USC and on the way back to the crib, they discussed the school and their visit. Razah was only half listening, because while the visit had been good, it had also been an eye opener, and now all he could think about was the paper waiting for him.

They say I couldn't play football, I was too small.
They say I couldn't play basketball, I wasn't tall,
They say I couldn't bag chicks at all.
Now Every Day of My Life I Ball!

Michaela L. Rivera

The next morning before the conference, Mizz and Razah talked about the visit.

"So how was it kid?" Mizz asked.

"Damn, sonn, that shit was hard. I don't know if I wanna go there though."

"I don't think it will be a good idea." Mizz said in a some what serious tone.

"Me neither." Razah said laughing, knowing exactly what he meant.

"On some real shit, I hope there is some bitches at the conference today."

"For real sonn, for real." They dapped each other up and went off to get dressed.

Cameras were waiting for them as they approached the conference. News stations and reporters called out their names trying to score an interview. It was all a little overwhelming for them since it was their first time on camera. They stopped and gave a few comments to the reporters then they headed inside.

As they made their way towards the podium, they stopped dead in their tracks. Standing at the podium was the most beautiful girl they had ever seen. She had jet black hair that barely touched her shoulders, big brown eyes, and nice full lips. She was wearing a form fitting black dress that perfectly accentuated her well-toned body and natural curves. The hint of perfectly tanned cleavage that was exposed by her blouse completed the picture. They looked at each other in denial, both thinking the same thing.

"Damn, ain't she the shit." She stepped up to the mic and introduced herself as Michaela L. Rivera. They sat

They say I couldn't play football, I was too small.
They say I couldn't play basketball, I wasn't tall,
They say I couldn't bag chicks at all.
Now Every Day of My Life I Ball!

down in their respective seats behind her; neither of them
missed that the view from behind was just as nice. Mizz
and Razah smiled each other as she turned to introduce
them.

"For the first time in the National Honor Society
history, we have a student athlete with the IQ of Mr.
Barack Obama. He is a number one picked basketball
player and 4.0 student who is taking college courses. I'm
pleased to introduce Mizzier "Mizz" Stenson." She said
clapping her hands.

"Thanks, I would like to speak to you after." He
whispered to her as he joined her at the podium.

"Thank you," he began as the audience gave him a
standing ovation. "First, I would like to thank God, my
family, and my sidekick Myshawn. I would also like to
thank Ms. Michaela Rivera for that introduction."

After the conference, Mizz and Razah mingled with
the crowd as they looked for Ms. Rivera. Razah caught
sight of her standing by the door and he called Mizz over.

"Damn Mizz, there she is. Watch this." Razah said,
walking up to her. He cleared his throat and put on his best
game face.

"Hey ma, what's good?"

"Hey ma, what's good?" She shook her head. "I'm
not your ma, you clown."

"Clown owe, word. I guess you're one of those angry
bitches, huh? A feminist?" Razah shot back.

"What?! That's no way to talk to a lady."

"I'm sorry, madam." He said backing off.

"Sonn, chill, chill." Mizz said walking up as Razah
turned and walked away.

They say I couldn't play football, I was too small.
They say I couldn't play basketball, I wasn't tall,
They say I couldn't bag chicks at all.
Now Every Day of My Life I Ball!

Michaela stood there in disbelief. "Wow."

"He didn't mean nothing by that. He been going through some things as of late, so."

"Well, you need to check him before."

"Baby, baby, don't let nobody steal your joy. Now, can I talk to you for a minute? Let's start all over."

She rolled her eyes. "Okay, go ahead."

"Excuse me. I'm sorry to bother you, but you're breath-taking. You're the most beautiful and the sexiest woman I have ever seen in my life."

She laughed.

"Why you laughing?" he said defensively.

"That was corny."

"No it wasn't. You were trippin' when my man called you ma. What is it?"

"So what if I was like 'damn dude you hot, ooooooh, my God I had to say something to you', would you believe me?"

"Um, um, yea."

"You're too funny. I have to go. Maybe I'll see you tonight at the award ceremony." She said as she turned to walk away.

"Yea, I will be looking for you." They headed their separate ways both hoping that they would run into each other again.

Mizz saw Razah standing by the refreshment table. He made his way over and picked up a cookie. Razah, already knowing the answer, asked, "What happen sonn?"

"Probably get at her later at the award shit."

"Sonn, everything is straight wit the situation."

"Word? Everything, everything?"

They say I couldn't play football, I was too small.
They say I couldn't play basketball, I wasn't tall,
They say I couldn't bag chicks at all.
Now Every Day of My Life I Ball!

"Sonn, we good business."

"Let's get it poppin'."

They headed back to the crib to check on the crew and to get ready for the ceremony. All of the paper had been counted and they had already started packing up the bins. Everything looked straight so they got dressed in their best threads and headed out. After they arrived at the conference, they immediately started looking for Michaela and soon saw her standing with one of her friends. She spotted them and motioned for them to come over. She introduced her friend, Tess, to them just as the lights flickered letting them know that the ceremony was about to start. They all agreed to meet later. While Michaela made her way to the stage, Mizz and Razah went looking for their seats. After the ceremony, Tess bumped into Mizz. "Hey, you look lost. Can I be of any assistance?" Tess offered with a smile.

"I'm looking for Michaela."

"Oh, you like her huh?"

"Why you think that?" he asked trying to sound surprised at the question.

"Cuz most dudes sweat her. Look at her, she's hot."

"I would expect you to say that." He said as he saw Michaela walking up the stairs. He grabbed Razah to speak with Tess. "I got someone for you to meet."

"How you doin' madam?" Razah said looking Tess up and down.

"Madam?" she said, shaking her head a little.

Mizz hurried up the stairs and caught up with Michaela at the top.

"Good evening Ms. Lady." Mizz said trying to catch his breath. It wasn't the stairs that had gotten to him, it was her

They say I couldn't play football, I was too small.
They say I couldn't play basketball, I wasn't tall,
They say I couldn't bag chicks at all.
Now Every Day of My Life I Ball!

stunning good looks and the chance to speak with her again that had him a little choked up.

"Please don't call me that. I want you to look at me as your colleague. So, tell me something, how does it feel being the most popular kid in the world right now?"

"I didn't come up here to talk about that. I came up here to get to know you and express my "g"."

"Oh really? Well, let me hear it, but first, I gotta tell you something. I'm not looking for a relationship and I don't date guys on the National Honor Society."

"Then I'm your friend and I quit." Mizz said, without any hesitation.

"You can't quit, I need you." She said, her eyes and voice softening as she took a step closer. "Wait, let me see. You got something on your lip."

"What is it?"

She leaned in and kissed him.

"You seducing me? Damn you got game." He said as she stepped back again.

"Let me tell you something. When I seduce, Mizzier you will know," and with that, she kissed him again.

They say I couldn't play football, I was too small.
They say I couldn't play basketball, I wasn't tall,
They say I couldn't bag chicks at all.
Now Every Day of My Life I Ball!

The Director

A few minutes later, he went to go find Razah. Razah had stopped talking to Tess and was engaged in what seemed to be a pretty deep conversation with some random dude. Mizz walked up to them and Razah introduced him. The dude, it turned out, was a movie director and had been following Mizz and Razah in the news for quite some time. He wanted to do a movie about their life and their journey over the next year. The boys said they would think about it and get back to him. The director gave them his card and invited them to check out his studio the next day. They were down with the idea and he agreed to pick them up at their hotel in the morning.

The next morning, Mizz and Razah waited in the lobby for the director. He arrived a few minutes late in a black Escalade with full tinted windows and the freshest rims that they had ever seen. They climbed in and the inside was decked out with TV screens, a little mini bar, and the plush leather seats. They were riding in style.

When they arrived at the studio, they were given the royal treatment. 'We could get used to this,' Mizz and Razah thought to themselves. The director, who asked the boys to call him Chase, brought them onto the set of his latest movie, a slasher film being done in the classic style. Mizz said he had always wondered how the makeup and special effects worked, so Chase took them into a back room where several masks were lined up each next to a computer. Over the next hour, he explained to them in detail the process of taking a person and turning them into someone or something else. Mizz, who had always been fascinated with this shit, took mental notes.

They say I couldn't play football, I was too small.
They say I couldn't play basketball, I wasn't tall,
They say I couldn't bag chicks at all.
Now Every Day of My Life I Ball!

After the tour, Chase dropped them back at the hotel and told them to call him when they were interested in discussing his idea further. The agreed and went off to get ready to return to New York.

They say I couldn't play football, I was too small.
They say I couldn't play basketball, I wasn't tall,
They say I couldn't bag chicks at all.
Now Every Day of My Life I Ball!

Keepin' it "G"

A few hours later they sat on the plane and chatted
about everything.
"Sonn, so you bagged Shorty or what?" Razah asked
really wanting some detail. .
"She straight. She was bullshitting." Mizz replied.
"You know how them bitches do."
"I feel you. You think you going to beat?"
"Maybe kid. I ain't stressin' that bitch sonn. Far as
I'm concerned, M.O.B." He got serious again. "Cali was
Cali and we should leave it at that, feel me?"
"I feel your "g" kid. That's why you my nigg."
Razah sat back in his chair and put on his headphones.
Mizz sat looking out the window thinking about the events
of the past few days. Real paper was waiting for them back
home. No more bull shit. When they touched down, Razah
immediately hit up Leak to see if everything was cool.
"Sonn, holla at me." Razah said into the phone.
"You young niggas are geniuses."
"So, we good?"
"Yes sir. Meet me at my spot."
"Ok, holla back." Razah hung up and looked at Mizz
who was eager to know what was up.
"What's good?" he asked.
"IGHTTTTTTT!!! RAZAH!!!"
"True story?"
"True story," Razah assured Mizz. "We gotta go to
Leak's crib and handle that."
"We there."
As they approached Leak's house, the two of them
remained cool, calm, and confident as if nothing had

They say I couldn't play football, I was too small.
They say I couldn't play basketball, I wasn't tall,
They say I couldn't bag chicks at all.
Now Every Day of My Life I Ball!

happened. They climbed out of the cab and walked up to the old run-down duplex that Leak called home. Now it wasn't that Leak was poor. No, he had plenty of green, but he had learned a long time ago that one could use their money for many things and he just didn't see the point in spending it on his crib. Besides, he had to keep close to his clientele.

"What up niggas?" Leak said as he invited them inside.

"Chillin." they said in unison.

"Did you do what I ask?" Razah continued.

"Of course cuz, of course," replied Leak.

"Where the dough? I know nigga you didn't bring the shit over here as hot as the spot is." Mizz said.

"Hell no. You two niggas ain't the only one that smart" laughed Leak.

"I told Leak to go to a storage spot. He had some couches, chairs, tables, and shit. So when he left his Shorty's job, he went to the storage spot," assured Razah.

"Oh, sonn. You surprise me more and more."

"We will go there right now and get a few dollars to hold us down for a minute so we won't be obvious coming back and forth over here," suggested Razah.

"Yea you right," agreed Mizz.

They say I couldn't play football, I was too small.
They say I couldn't play basketball, I wasn't tall,
They say I couldn't bag chicks at all.
Now Every Day of My Life I Ball!

Time for Change

The days passed by quickly and soon the end of the football season drew near. And with basketball season just around the corner, it would soon be time for Mizz to showcase his stuff. Mizz looked at the calendar and smiled; tomorrow was the first day of the preseason. It had been too long since he last crossed some dude and dropped a trey on his head. He couldn't wait to be back out on the court.

"Yo sonn, your season is pretty much here." Razah said coming up behind Mizz and putting a hand on his shoulder.

"I know sonn. I hope to have a season like yours B. You just have the stats left. You set madd records."

"No doubt, but we got the paper so what you going to do about your idea?"

"I know sonn. Get Leak and his people together and let's meet later on tonight in the abandoned building on Bishop."

"No doubt."

Later that night, Leak and a few of his goons met up with Mizz and Razah at the abandoned spot on Bishop. Tucked away in a remote section of the neighborhood with broken out windows and decorated with graffiti on all of its walls, both inside and out, the old warehouse had been abandoned for years and served as a perfect spot for the kind of business transactions that were best done in secret.

Mizz pulled open a makeshift door that was nothing more than an oversized piece of plywood and led them inside.

"Damn sonn. You don't trust a muthafucker." Leaked

They say I couldn't play football, I was too small.
They say I couldn't play basketball, I wasn't tall,
They say I couldn't bag chicks at all.
Now Every Day of My Life I Ball!

look around. "No bugs in this shit. You're a smart young muthafucker kid, choosing this spot though sonn, abandoned building in shit." Mizz gathered everyone around. "Well, let's get started." Mizz stopped and looked at one of the crew. "Oh shit Meneto. What brings you down here cuzin? I haven't seen you in years. You must like broke niggas, Meneto! What would make a high price insurance agent like yourself come and hang wit house dumb niggas like us?"

"I'm no coon; its basic common sense and arithmetic. It's a difference from them paying me $1,000 a week and you paying me $10,000 a week." Meneto replied. He had long since left the street game and had gone legit, getting a job as a salesman for a well-respected insurance firm. But when he had heard about this opportunity to make some real change, he decided to rethink his current situation.

"Good, cuz you gotta rob and steal to get ahead fucking wit George W. Bush, the way he fucked up this economy. For real kid!" Mizz saw this was the time to lay it down for everyone. "Anyways," he began, "there is an enormous growin' of niggas wit no paper, disenfranchised. Then these Republican niggas act like the shit don't exist." Mizz continued.

"Meanwhile, the corporate muthafuckers get richer." Razah joined in.

"And the middle class and poor don't get a fuckin' thing." Meneto agreed.

"When shit like this go down, muthafuckers wanna get high, dumb high, and wild fast and please believe my niggas this," Mizz said holding up holding up what looked like a piece of candy, "is going to do it and make us rich and its completely legal."

They say I couldn't play football, I was too small.
They say I couldn't play basketball, I wasn't tall,
They say I couldn't bag chicks at all.
Now Every Day of My Life I Ball!

"What, this look like a peppermint your moms would give you in church." Leak's girlfriend, Chantress, said.
Not yet wanting to get into the specifics, Mizz moved ahead ignoring her comment. "The white folks, white collar crime, Madoff, the great get money hustles Freddie Myers, Rick Ross, Guy Fisher, Rich Porter, Rafer Edmonds, and especially the last crew to do it, like no other than **BMF**..

Black Mafia Family, shout out to Big Meech, hold your head. They all shown us the way. The shit is hard how they freaked it. But fam, we doing this shit different, all of us working on the beeper, cell phone. You change the product you change the marketing strategy. We're done worrying about territory or what corner we got or what project. The game ain't about that no more, it's about product. We got the best product and we going to sell no matter where we are, PRODUCT MUTHAFUCKERS!! PRODUCT! Check this out, half the real estate twice the product, the territory don't mean shit if the product is wack.

Muthafuckers be having the projects and corners. For example, niggas play b ball here in the states, but go overseas to get that cake. Territory ain't shit. It's about product and niggas we got the product. We taking this game to another level, and thinking like some white collar corporate muthafuckers, not some ghetto ass niggas on the fuckin corner." Mizz said now sounding more and more like a leader with every word. "So the concept is this basically, the whole family has to be put together as a black army and we going to take over the east and west coast and walk on this nation and walk on this racist power structure and we going to say to the whole dam government stick em up mutha fucka this a hold up and we going to take what's ours!!! But we going to do it in a way and change the game.

They say I couldn't play football, I was too small.
They say I couldn't play basketball, I wasn't tall,
They say I couldn't bag chicks at all.
Now Every Day of My Life I Ball!

You feel me, not like some of the other crews that did come up cuz wit time brothers got smarter and wise. For instance, Y.B.I Young Boys inc, B.G.F Black Gorilla Family,

Bloods, Crips, Vice Lords, Gansta Disciples, Junior Black Mafia. The list goes on and on but again the crew that did it like no other was Black Mafia Family BMF. We need to take a little bit from all of these crews and build our empire to the fullest. Failure is not an option. Everyone in our family will move like brothers and sisters and will move as ONE. Everyone will prosper in their own way, but it all starts with the head of the body, the leader. So a good leader", Mizz, speaking in third person just in case, "has good people behind him. But if you a fuck boy leader, you going to have fuck boys behind you, not loyal muthafuckas, just straight grimy niggaz.

A real leader takes the good wit the bad and shows you how to come up out of it.. That's the meaning of a real leader and it formulates into Black enterprise. Trust me, there will never be another crew like this one and if there is they wont be black, not in this life time. Like I said, BMF was the last, and they don't know it, but they passed the torch to us and we gladly taking it. On the other hand, what's important is that we all came into this together, we all making money, but money aint nothing if we don't got each other and we not going to fall out over no bitches!! No disrespect to the ladies in here, but again we aint falling out over no hoes.

We hitting them all, you hit my bitch I hit your bitch every girl fair game unless its your wifey!! Let me repeat again, we not falling out over no bitches. Look at all the kinds of different niggaz in this room. Dark niggaz, light niggaz, short niggaz, tall niggaz, nasty niggaz, fat niggaz,

They say I couldn't play football, I was too small.
They say I couldn't play basketball, I wasn't tall,
They say I couldn't bag chicks at all.
Now Every Day of My Life I Ball!

big heads niggaz, braids, dreads, niggaz wit beards, bald
head niggaz, and you all got money and we cant get along
cuz of some trick, hell no!! Not happening. Plus it's to
many bitches out there, you got money so you can have
your pick of hoes. Fat bitches, ghetto bitches, hood rats,
white bitches, models, bitches wit weaves, whatever you
want. But please, I' m a emphasize, I don't want no
beefing, no drama, just business; no unnecessary attention
to us.

One thing for sure, you wanna trick, watch your
purchases cuz it will turn against you. That's what them
people want you to do!!!! If you wanna get anywhere and
get any real money, don't fuck wit the street dealers. Like I
said, you change the product you change the marketing
strategy. You take out one of them niggas. It's a thousand
of them muthafuckers right there in that place. We going to
fuck wit niggas that have clout, something to lose; not
Willie and Nut Nutt getting shot up in the hallway over a
dime bag. Nah we ain't going out like that. We going to
fuck wit niggas that can make us rich and then turn around
and we supply them. Feel me! Here is the scoop," Mizz
reached behind him and took a board with a bunch of
names and pictures on it. "Here we go. Check this out,
Willie Johnson, he is the middle man. He supplies the
niggas who supplies the streets. This muthafucker gets his
shit from the importer Jerome Massifield, he is the number
one importer on the east coast. Fifty percent of all the
drugs in New England goes thru this guy. He is able to do
this cuz his step-father Carlos Rodiquez Gomez is the first
cousin of the Latin, self-promoting, and influential
politician Felix Sanchez."

Mizz said pointing to one of the pictures on the

They say I couldn't play football, I was too small.
They say I couldn't play basketball, I wasn't tall,
They say I couldn't bag chicks at all.
Now Every Day of My Life I Ball!

board. "Sanchez is the nigga that helps Massifield get the drugs into the country. Our goal is to get at these niggas and have them buy from us like how the nigga Frank Lucas did to mob in an American gangster, smell me?" Mizz stopped speaking for a minute to get the reaction from his friend and potential business associates.

"So we going after the Felix nigga first?" asked Razah.

"Not right now, the muthafucker too big Sonn. That's like saying Jordan versus CJ Miles." Replied Mizz.

"Who?" Razah asked

Mizz continued. "Exactly, but it is if we can get to the step, Sonn and holla at the cousin and hurt him financially. Now my niggas, that would be good for us and make a name in high places, feel me? But everyone listen, we get to Johnson and then Massifield, in that order. Why? Cuz it protects us, and word of mouth and money is a muthafucker. Fam, we goin' to change the whole damn game. Just imagine keys of this shit in worldwide distribution. Plus we doing us here in this spot its crazy. We will have loyal customers. We going to set up lab here on Bronson, here to make the product. Jesse, you could find the two spots on Bronson wit the real estate shit, ya know. And hook up the PC shit cuz that's what you do.

Watch out for the workers, money, product. Leak, we need muscle to watch out for the hating ass niggas and screen out the customers. Soon we going to need look outs to holla on every block. One place to make the product and another place to collect our money. Sonn, the world is ours. But my niggas these are designer drugs. Shit it's not like ecstasy, crystal meth, or pills. What's crazy is that this drug is completely legal and absolutely safe. Niggas will go

They say I couldn't play football, I was too small.
They say I couldn't play basketball, I wasn't tall,
They say I couldn't bag chicks at all.
Now Every Day of My Life I Ball!

to work and do their job better than they did the muthafucker when they were sober or straight. My niggas all of you or most of you have sold crack! What is crack?

Some of our family is on crack, true story. We all grew up in this shit whether we like it or not, we street niggas real talk. But crack is an addiction that people can't kick; some do but mostly niggas can't kick and it's a lost cause. Ever since crack came on the scene in the late 80's early 90's, it's been going strong and getting stronger by the minute. Crack fries the brain and the sex drive, forget about it. And in my opinion a crack addiction is worse than nicotine.

People can't cope and the after effect, we already know the result. The shit is dumb illegal and you can get it on any block and shit corner. For real though, I have been taking classes and worked in a pharmacy the last two summers, this peppermint candy is a chemical barrier. It increases your attention, energy, contemplative powers yet with a segue and smooth transformation. Inside the red strips, that is where the shit takes place and you feel like you about to blast off. It's completely legal and I'm the only one that knows how to make it. My niggas this whole east coast is ours."

"This is an unbelievable plan my nigga." Razah said almost clapping.

"One more thing," Mizz continued. "My niggas you ever see a crack baby, a new born crack baby, seven hours old yelling and screaming cuz it's all fucked up. The baby, probably in the next year or two, will not be able to do things on time like walking, talking, crawling or even laughing, cuz all the bullshit drugs that mother did. The baby has major physical and mental deformities. It is

They say I couldn't play football, I was too small.
They say I couldn't play basketball, I wasn't tall,
They say I couldn't bag chicks at all.
Now Every Day of My Life I Ball!

definitely dyslexic and who the fuck knows what else. If the baby is lucky to even go to school it can't learn and has temper trips all the time. Most likely by the time the kid is ten years old, it is already in the foster care system. Like I said before, the majority of you here have hustled crack and still doing it now. My niggas where we come from there are mad babies like that that cuz these niggas are bringing that bullshit in this country. And the majority of our people is being murdered before they get the chance to live their own life. That's why we going to change the game. Damn!!! Drugs."

They say I couldn't play football, I was too small.
They say I couldn't play basketball, I wasn't tall,
They say I couldn't bag chicks at all.
Now Every Day of My Life I Ball!

The Black Enterprise

Mizz held up the piece of candy again and laid out his business plan.

"I know you're wondering how we going to get this on and popp'n. Hear me, out you wont be disappointed. From this point on, loyalty and trust will define our family, not the love of money.

Its always Business, never personal. The whole operation is called The Black Enterprise. The Black Enterprise is a fortune 500 Company made up of black geniuses. The model is I failed ova and ova again therefore I succeed . This means, there is no more room for failure so no bad decision exists in the   Black Enterprise. The company will be broken down like this.

You will have to punch a clock with shifts like, day shift 7a.m. to 3p.m, evening shift 3p.m. to 11p.m., and over night 11p.m. to 7p.m. This will be at all our locations and I will appoint Lieutenants for each shift." At this, Mizz saw among them those who would be his first picks but opted to save that news for after the meeting. "There is no reason wit our product we won't be able to sell six to ten keys a day.

Never, and I mean never write shit down. And at the end of the week you'll pay all who worked at each location, $1,500 for the week. Trust, we're gonna monopolize the game because we can.

We're the only ones who know how to make it and we're gonna supply the whole Tri-State with this candy. So what we're gonna do is give our Columbia connect 300 keys as a test," pointing to one of his family crew members for emphasis, "if everything goes according

They say I couldn't play football, I was too small.
They say I couldn't play basketball, I wasn't tall,
They say I couldn't bag chicks at all,
Now Every Day of My Life I Ball!

to plan, and he proves to be worthy, then we will supply him whatever he wants. For example, another 100 keys, 50 keys, 25 keys, 10 keys.

Supply and demand will bring in millions of dollars, enough to fill my crib and razahs crib combined! My family, this is gonna happen fast, like no one's ever seen before. It's not a stretch to say that we will be the largest distributor in New York City and on the East Coast if everything is to a T, this plan could easily be pulling in 200 million dollars a year ." Certain he had clearly stated their motivation and earning power, Mizz again raised the candy in front of them and signaled the meeting had come to an end.

When Mizz wasn't playing ball, he was giving samples of his wonder candy out on his block. When people started coming back and just had to have more, he went from 5 dollars to 10 to 20 a pop. With business popping he designated locations to the family members and close friends he had brought in with his impassioned speech and solid business plan. With this candy being more popular than cocaine, crack, herion, exexex and with a lot of the local dope dealers getting bagged, Mizz and his crew took over blocks during the early stages. Mizz and Razah used warehouses and abandoned buildings to package the candy for distribution.

This was looking like a regular drug operation.The runners were selling ounces, half ounces, 50s, 20s, 10s round the clock. It wasn't unusual to have 50 to 60 transactions an hour. On each block, when the runner got low on his supply, he'd go to his car and beep the horn six times signaling the supplier to drop more candy for him out the window of the project building . Lookouts were posted

They say I couldn't play football, I was too small.
They say I couldn't play basketball, I wasn't tall,
They say I couldn't bag chicks at all.
Now Every Day of My Life I Ball!

on the roof tops. Leak, who was the most trusted out of the group had his girl rent several apartments in the projects in her name where they held large amounts of money for the crew. She and Leak were their main carriers for their distribution activities and for quality control, using their Columbian connections. For instance, since Mizz was the only one who knew how to make the product, they did a test run with Mizz giving Leak's girl seventeen keys of candy which she hid in her luggage and she'd come back with a small lump sum of money compared to what they were about to receive.

The Columbian had to almost test the feedback from the loyal buyers and other distributors. The next run was for 300 keys worth 3 million dollars, like I said it will be. Leak transported the keys along with his girl who rented the U-Haul to travel around the country to meet the Columbian connection in Portland, Oregon. Though the candy took over cocaine in popularity and it was creating a drug epidemic in its own right, no one knew it was, by nature of the formula, completely legal. It was widely available in every ghetto and suburb. With business growing, Mizz's organization grew with it, and a large amount of the candy was being made and supplied in the tri-state. Mizz was able to specify and allocate a large amount of the candy because he made it for retail and wholesale.

They say I couldn't play football, I was too small.
They say I couldn't play basketball, I wasn't tall,
They say I couldn't bag chicks at all.
Now Every Day of My Life I Ball!

Mizz entrusted only his family and closest friends with the cutting and wrapping of the candy for all sales.

They say I couldn't play football, I was too small.
They say I couldn't play basketball, I wasn't tall,
They say I couldn't bag chicks at all.
Now Every Day of My Life I Ball!

What's Really Good

Mizz and Razah met up the next morning and headed to school. Mizz couldn't wait for the day to end and his first practice to begin. He missed his team, his coach, and his court, and this season held the promise of greatness. Razah tapped him on the shoulder shaking him from his thought.

"Sonn, it's finally here kid."

"I know sonn. It seems like I was just at your first game and now we bout to start fam." Mizz said thinking about the season.

"You deadly sonn."

Mizz's tone became serious. "Sonn, I needed to tell you something from the other day kid. Word, well bro we have been thru thick and thin, I love you nigga no homo. That's why the money we make with this other shit we will be straight even if neither of us go pro. Sonn, I will send the money we make to this country in Africa, 'member when I studied there a couple of summers ago? Well, I met this dude that owns a store. We always kept in contact.

Well you know it's cheaper there so I have a contract with a store that I buy and rent things, word sonn. They will deposit the money in a bank; then they will intern give me a loan that I don't have to file taxes for years to come. Word!" But anyway," he continued. "Cuz like I was saying, just wanted you to know family."

He changed the topic back to basketball. "Of course kid, we start at four today no basketballs. Then tomorrow we play, pick up so those niggas get one more day before I bust that ass, feel me?" Mizz said mimicking a cross over.

"IGHT sonn, Word! I love you too nigga no homo."

They say I couldn't play football, I was too small.
They say I couldn't play basketball, I wasn't tall,
They say I couldn't bag chicks at all.
Now Every Day of My Life I Ball!

Razah nodded.

"Word!" Mizz thumped his chest.

"What's really good though, my nigga, is with the other shit. That plan you got is on and poppin'." Razah knew that their wait for the paper would soon be over.

"I'm going online at the library, get one of the kids to sign in and order the shit and get it sent to the school. Coach thinks it the gun that shooting machine shit, but Sonn I ordered that last week and it came in, just sittin' at the crib waiting and shit." Mizz had found the perfect place to hide the machine, right where nobody would think to look.

"You one smart nigga fam, for real B."

"Word!" Mizz replied.

Razah changed the subject hoping to get some juice. "By the way sonn, you been fuckin' wit shorty, the bitch from the convention and shit?"

"Ooooooh, you mean the fly shorty Michaela?" Mizz smiled thinking about their kiss.

"Yea sonn, that fly bitch."

"I speak to sexy every now and again, but nothing serious tho'. She asked for a schedule and shit."

"Where she from kid? She from Brooklyn Park Slope and shit." Razah asked and then answered his own question.

"Word! How you know kid? It said it in the program or some shit?"

"Yea my nigga."

"One. The Brooklyn bitches crazy tho' sonn." Mizz said thinking about a girl from Brooklyn that he fucked with the year before.

"A bitch that bad B, can do whatever she want."

> *They say I couldn't play football, I was too small.*
> *They say I couldn't play basketball, I wasn't tall,*
> *They say I couldn't bag chicks at all.*
> *Now Every Day of My Life I Ball!*

"Word sonn!!" Mizz agreed.

"Word!!" They laughed, dapped each other up, and agreed to get at each other after school.

Later that day, Mizz met up with his coach to discuss the upcoming season. But even with what could be the season of his life so far, just around the corner, his mind kept going back to the plan and to the paper.

"Mizz, what's good player? I heard you the best thing since sliced bread." The coach said thinking about a potential championship.

"Coach, you crazy. Just workin' hard." Mizz said.

"I know buddy, I just want you to stay focused. There are going to be a lot of haters and leaches trying to get on and get next to you."

"Thanks, Coach. Not only are you my coach, you're my friend."

"Thanks. I want you to lead this year and run preseason training and keep the team focused and ready. There will be a scrimmage next week, then the first game the following week. It's moving fast. The first game is on TV. How's your sidekick?" coach said thinking about Razah and his upcoming game.

"He's chillin'." Mizz shrugged.

"They got state championship game this weekend, huh?"

"Yea, they should win. He got mad schools after him tho', more than me."

"Bullshit," Coach chuckled. "You and he got the same schools. I watch ESPN. "

Mizz laughed out loud. "You right. Just makin' sure you paying attention." Mizz changed the subject, his mind still focused on the plan. "I ordered the gun, it should be here

They say I couldn't play football, I was too small.
They say I couldn't play basketball, I wasn't tall,
They say I couldn't bag chicks at all.
Now Every Day of My Life I Ball!

next week."

"All right. Well, kid just wanted to holla at you. See you next week in practice." Coach patted him on the shoulder and left.

"Ok, Coach. Thanks man, see you then." Mizz called after him.

The weekend finally arrived bringing with it all of the hype that talent like Razah's commands. He was expected to bring home the championship and everyone was on hand to witness this phenomenon make history. The stadium was filled with mad scouts and TV cameras. Razah's mom couldn't believe that all of this attention was for her son. She felt a deep sense of pride flood over her as she heard the announcer introduce her son.

"Razah is leading the nation in the categories of rushing yards, kick-off return yards, and touchdowns. He is by far the #1 rated prospect in the nation. I haven't seen a back like this since a combination of Barry Sanders and Reggie Bush. This kid is serious and he's only a sophomore." The game started and the crowd went wild as Razah returned the opening kickoff 98 yards for a touchdown. His mom joined the crowd as they started the familiar chant of Razah! Razah! Razah! Mizz and Mikey went nuts waving their signs yelling right along with the crowd. Razah didn't stop there as he led his team to a 28-7 victory rushing for 325 yards and running for 3 touchdowns, breaking all high school records for a single game. His teammates carried him off the field on their shoulders as scores of reporters tried to be the first to speak with him.

The next day was Sunday and it was Razah's time to chill. He sat eating breakfast, thinking about the game

They say I couldn't play football, I was too small.
They say I couldn't play basketball, I wasn't tall,
They say I couldn't bag chicks at all.
Now Every Day of My Life I Ball!

when Mizz showed up at his door. As he got up to answer, he realized he hadn't gotten a chance to speak with him after the game. Mizz was still smiling. "Yo!! Razah kid, you nasty.""Thanks bro." Razah smiled.

"You were surrounded last night. Couldn't get to you kid. Damn B, you're that nigga fam." Mizz said proudly.

"Your mom dukes was in the building too, sonn."

"No doubt. It felt good too." Razah thought about how great it felt to see her in the stands rooting for him. He then changed the subject. "How's practice been going kid?"

"I've been dragging niggas. It's real light, you know how I do. Same shit different toilet, word!" answered Mizz."Word! I saw Leak at the game."

"He chillin'. He was wit the Goon Squad."

"I peeped it."

"We bout to get it on and poppin' as soon as the season starts." Mizz started going over the plan. "I spoke wit Jesse. He almost got the spots, waiting for niggas to move out and shit. Chantress and Leak getting the muscle together so we should be straight in the next few weeks kid. Word, oh I forgot to tell you, shit got delivered so we straight."

"Word sonn."

"Word, trying to be like you my nigg, word! Have you been back to the storage sonn?" asked Mizz.

"Fuck no," Razah answered sounding shocked. "We going together right?"

"Right."

"I spoke to niggas and they said we straight." Razah recalled the conversation with his cousin. "That shit been on the news crazy. They said no leads to anything, it's like the whole thing never happened."

They say I couldn't play football, I was too small.
They say I couldn't play basketball, I wasn't tall,
They say I couldn't bag chicks at all,
Now Every Day of My Life I Ball!

"Say word sonn." Mizz shook his head.

"Word!"

"Razahhhhhhhhhhh cuzin. That shit is hard B."

"Bust it. They trying to trace the calls to the security niggas tho', fam." Razah cocked his head as he recounted what his cousin had told him.

"One, word?" Mizz sounded worried.

"Word sonn. There is no way they can trace the number or if they do wit all the technology bullshit, the phone is in the sewer and the sim card is wit me." Razah said assuring Mizz and himself that they were straight.

"Guard that shit wit your life cuzin for real sonn, word cuz." Mizz's tone got serious.

"Word."

"That shit was gangster tho', how it went down tho cuz!" Mizz replayed the heist over again in his mind.

"Word Razah!"

"Word Razah!" He looked at the clock. His mom was due home soon. "But I will holla later. My moms doing something nice cuz of the game sonn. Word!"

"Ok B, one." Mizz got up to leave.

"One."

The next day on the way to school, they saw Murdock on the block chillin' and he told the niggas to get in the whip. He wanted to talk. Murdock was a little guy but had worked out most of his life, so no one fucked with him. Mizz and Razah got into the car to see what he wanted.

"Yo sonn, that shit was hard. The plan and everything, I was thinking on how we can..." Murdock started but before he could finish his sentence, Razah screamed.

"Yo!" and reached to blast the music in the car.

"Cuzo, stop the car and let's take a walk." Mizz

They say I couldn't play football, I was too small.
They say I couldn't play basketball, I wasn't tall,
They say I couldn't bag chicks at all.
Now Every Day of My Life I Ball!

demanded. "Yo sonn, come on B. You're new muscle." Mizz said as they got out of the car.

"What's the rules sonn?" Razah looked at Murdock almost staring him down.

"I know the rule." Murdock said defensively.

"Say it." Mizz wasn't fucking around.

"Don't talk in the car or on the phone or to anyone that ain't down wit us. But it's just you niggas." Murdock answered as Razah just stood there looking at him.

"Ok, I got it." Murdock put his hands motioning surrender. They got back in the car and Murdock dropped them off at school.

"Good luck today dude, do work." He said as they got out of the car.

"Yea, good look. You do the same." Mizz said. As he walked up to school he turned and watched Murdock drive off. "That's one dumb ass nigga," he said to Razah as they walked into school. Razah nodded in agreement and they headed off to class.

The season opener came and as expected, was jam packed with fans and reporters. ESPN was covering it and for the first time in his life, Mizz would be playing live on television. Every coach in the area eagerly waited to see what Mizz would bring in his first game. Mizz was hyped to be playing at the coliseum and couldn't wait for the game to start. During his warm-ups he scanned the crowd and spotted Razah, Leak, and their muscle. He then saw someone else he hadn't expected. 'Oh shit, its shorty, Michaela.' He said to himself his mind forgetting about the rest of the crowd and focusing on her. He looked over to make eye contact with Razah who was sitting behind the team's bench. After layups, as Mizz walked over to the

They say I couldn't play football, I was too small.
They say I couldn't play basketball, I wasn't tall,
They say I couldn't bag chicks at all.
Now Every Day of My Life I Ball!

bench to sit, he tapped Razah. "Sonn, look."

"Oh shit." Razah. said.

"Word B, she look dumb good cuzin." Mizz's mind had now completely forgotten about the game.

"Word sonn, she definitely a stallion."

"I'm droppin' 50 sonn." Mizz said with confidence.

"Say word sonn." Razah answered nodding.

"Word."

He walked out onto the court and before the opening tipoff made eye contact with Michaela. She winked, smiled, and waved while whispering 'good luck'. Mizz did not disappoint the record crowd that had come out to see him. Toward the end of the 3rd quarter, he had 43 points, 10 assists, and 10 rebounds. He was a fierce competitor and a driving force and could easily have been playing pro ball.

As he sat on the bench waiting for the fourth quarter to begin, Mizz looked to the stands and saw Jesse point to him and then whisper to Leak and Sanity. They all hugged. He knew that Jesse had found the spots. Razah tapped him on the shoulder.

"Sonn, I believe we good. I'm going to walk over there and see what's up."

"No, stay here. You will draw too much attention to yourself and I don't know why those niggas over there doing that nut-ass shit, feel me?" Mizz's tone was serious.

"I know, you right" Razah nodded. "They trippin". I will handle them niggas after the game."

"Word!! See you later sonn at the crib."

The fourth quarter started and by the end Mizz had another 13 points giving him 56 for the game hitting 13 three pointers and breaking the record for the most in a single outing. He ended up with a triple double adding 12

They say I couldn't play football, I was too small.
They say I couldn't play basketball, I wasn't tall,
They say I couldn't bag chicks at all.
Now Every Day of My Life I Ball!

assists and 13 rebounds. After the game, as if he were already playing pro ball, he gave a press conference and sat down for interviews with ESPN and other TV stations that had covered the game. After the interviews he showered, left the locker room and ran into Michaela who had been waiting to see him.

"Wow, you a bad boy on that court. Excuse me, can I have your autograph?" she said playfully.

"Of course you can. That's all you want?" Mizz replied looking into her eyes.

"For now, fresh boy." She smiled as he laughed out loud. They walked and talked about the game while Razah was somewhere else talking to the crew about the rules. "Fellas, what's good? My nigga was killin' them word." He said.

"Ight, ight, word." They answered in unison.

Razah then got down to business. "Ok, let's keep it real, niggas! What the fuck was good wit you muthafuckers huggin' and pointing and shit? You remember the rules, no kind of anything. Be cool at all times. Niggas, we work too hard to get here, all of us. You're black and hardcore. This cannot happen again. We family, we won't self destruct, trust! Nothin' will bring us down. We will own this fuckin' city." Meanwhile, Mizz and Michaela continued to walk and get to know each other better.

"So what made you come to my game?" Mizz asked.

"I got an aunt that lives out here, so on the weekends I take the train from the city to come visit her. Her daughter is my best friend, plus how can I not come? Your face is on every magazine and TV station." She said touching his arm.

"Word!! I thought you forgot about me."

They say I couldn't play football, I was too small.
They say I couldn't play basketball, I wasn't tall,
They say I couldn't bag chicks at all.
Now Every Day of My Life I Ball!

"Nah, you was cool. I liked your style." She said.

"So you was feelin' my "g", ight!" Mizz said nodding confidently.

"You're a funny dude." Michaela said almost laughing.

"So how many dudes you fuck wit?"

"A few, nothin' serious."

"Ight, that's cool."

"And you?" She said raising her eyebrows.

"I'm chillin'. I got friends, same deal."

"Well it was good seeing you again. My aunt is waiting for me. I will see you around." Michaela turned to leave.

"Can I get a number, an address or something?" Mizz said almost begging.

"No! I'll see you again." She answered as she walked away.

"Ewhh!! Wow, you played me." Mizz said to himself watching her as she got into her aunt's car. As she drove off, he memorized the license plate number.

The next day, Michaela is relaxing when there is a knock at the door. 'Who can that be,' she thought as she looked through the peephole to see Mizz standing on her porch.

"Hey beautiful." He said as he waved at her.

Michaela opened the door. "Mizz, what the hell you doin' here? How you know where my aunt lives?"

"I know that it's crazy I just popped up here."

"What did you do, follow me here?"

"Hell no!" he answered. "Well nothin' like that sexy girl. I did memorize your aunt's license plate." Mizz looked down realizing how crazy it sounded.

"Dude, are you loony?"

"But I just wanted to give you tickets to the next

They say I couldn't play football, I was too small.
They say I couldn't play basketball, I wasn't tall,
They say I couldn't bag chicks at all,
Now Every Day of My Life I Ball!

game." He said holding out a few tickets.

"Oh that was nice of you, thanks." She looked at him as he stood there looking around her and into her house. "You looking all around like you tryin' to come in or something negro."

"Nah," he shrugged and then changed his mind. "I mean hell yeah, but if you don't want me to it's cool. If you're not busy, I really wouldn't mind."

"I'm not busy. You can come in." She said opening the door and stepping inside.

"You ight. You cool for real." He smiled.

"Yea, it's fine."

"I hope I'm not barging in."

"Too late for that, don't ya think?" She said cocking her head.

"Your aunt's crib is hard. Where is she?" he decided changing the subject would be a good idea.

"She took my cousin to a college tour. So I'm here house-sitting and feeding the pets."
She looked at him. "Ok, Mizz, question. Why is your black ass here?"

"You came to my game, I had career numbers, and I want your support. And I figured if I asked you to come to the next game, you would say yes. If not that game, maybe the next game till the next game became the right game."

"Aw, I see, a man who is not willing to take no for an answer. Persistant." She nodded.

"You never know how far it can get you. I see you're into fashion, huh?" He looked at her. She was dressed in tight black Armani jeans with a white Dolce t-shirt that accentuated her upper body perfectly.

"You know about fashion?" She asked sounding

They say I couldn't play football, I was too small.
They say I couldn't play basketball, I wasn't too tall,
They say I couldn't bag chicks at all.
Now Every Day of My Life I Ball!

surprised.

"A lil' something, feel me. Gucci, Prada, Armani, Coach, Louis Vuitton, True Religion, Dolce and Gabana, Vogue."

"Damn, you go boy. So you're like a Renaissance black man, basketball, honor society, stylist, presidential and shit."

"You can say that! There was a quote by a famous actor, 'The world is yours,' Wesley Snipes in New Jack City. I guess I live like that." Mizz said sounding a little too confident.

"Ooohh, ok Mizz. You dumb ass nigga "know" your actors and movies. It was Al Pacino in Scarface. Now you're tryin' too hard, clown." Michaela said as the expression on her face changed slightly.

Mizz laughed. "I'm startin' to feel you, Ms. Lady."

"Well, don't feel me too much."

"Ight, for real though, my family is having a little surprise party for Razah for winning the state championship game and I want you to come and chill with me. Maybe we can start to catch up and get to know each other better."

"Are you trying to ask me out Mizz?" "You can say that Ms. Lady, I definitely am."

"I'm not too sure." She said as she thought about what a date with Mizz would be like.

"I can't take no for an answer. It will be a great ending to a beautiful day. So what do you say?" Mizz said holding out his hands.

"Since you put it that way, ok ight." She couldn't believe she was agreeing to this.

"I will come pick you up 9ish, if that's cool?"

"Yea, Mizz, next time you intrude, call first cuz I

They say I couldn't play football, I was too small.
They say I couldn't play basketball, I wasn't tall,
They say I couldn't bag chicks at all.
Now Every Day of My Life I Ball!

know your black ass got the house number."

Mizz laughed. "You right, I got your number."

At the party the next night, Mizz waited for Michaela to arrive. He was determined to be on his game with her that night. When she walked in the door, it seemed as if every guy in the place stopped and looked. Dressed in a very low-cut Louis blouse and a pair of black Prada jeans that looked like second skin, she stood at the door looking for Mizz.

Mizz saw her and immediately made his way to her. He took her by the arm and led her over to introduce her to the fam. She saw Razah standing there and it was love, like nothing happened the first time they met.

"Congrats to you on the championship." She said to Razah making him smile.

"Thanks. I see you chillin' wit my man." Razah leaned in close. "You better treat him right."

"We chillin', he's cool." She said.

Seeing that all was copacetic, Mizz interrupted. "Aight, I see you two made up, no doubt."

"Yea, we straight." Razah caught the Mizz's cue and left them alone. They hung out for a little while longer until they decided to break out to spend a little time alone.

"You hungry? I know a pizza shop we can go to." There wasn't much food at the party and Mizz was feeling pretty hungry.

"Cool, I'm starving." They made their way to the shop where they sat and talked about the season, the honor society, and even a little bit about fashion. He learned about what she liked and what her hopes were going forward. Mizz felt the chemistry between them starting to grow. An hour later Mizz walked her up to her aunt's door.

They say I couldn't play football, I was too small.
They say I couldn't play basketball, I wasn't tall,
They say I couldn't bag chicks at all.
Now Every Day of My Life I Ball!

They stood there for a few seconds while Mizz contemplated his next move. Michaela spoke first, breaking the silence.

"Thanks, I had a ball tonight."

"Me too." Mizz said looking into her eyes. "I haven't felt like this in a long time." He leaned and kissed her. She pulled back and looked at him. "Umm."

"My bad, I should break." Mizz said hoping that she wasn't really upset.

"Mizz, I had a good time, I just can't go out like that on the first date."

"I got you, I feel your "g"." Then they started kissing again. "Damn, my bad. I'll call you. Plus it's mad late." Mizz looked at his wrist like he was wearing a watch, which he wasn't.

"Yea you right, call me." She agreed while making a poor attempt to catch her breath.

"Fuck, I just wanna come in and talk." Mizz decided to take the chance to see what would happen.

She laughed, knowing that was the last thing he or she wanted to do. "Ok, just talk."

Mizz took her hand. "Is that cool, sexy?" She opened the door and pulled him inside. They immediately went upstairs to her room. She turned the stereo to some slow jams to set the mood. They kissed again and fell onto the bed. Mizz took his time and it was exactly what Michaela had hoped for. She was in love for real.

They say I couldn't play football, I was too small.
They say I couldn't play basketball, I wasn't tall,
They say I couldn't bag chicks at all.
Now Every Day of My Life I Ball!

The Morning After

The next morning Michaela woke to some delicious smells coming from the kitchen. "Damn, you really a Renaissance man making omelets and French toast." She said as she came downstairs looking even better than she had the night before. Mizz smiled. "For real though, I'm feeling you. I hope you don't look at me differently or feel we moved too quickly."

"Please, I wanted it to happen." She kissed him. "It takes two to tango."

"So that means I can see you again?" Mizz asked hopefully.

"Of course." She was surprised at the question.

"So you ain't going to front on me, then don't call me back, shit on me. I hate that bullshit. Anyway, you want something else?"

"Don't ask me that." She said as she walked up to him and pulled him in close.

"IGHT." He wasn't going to push the issue and feeling her body close to his, memories of past shit just disappeared. The next day, Mizz headed over to Razah's unable to stop thinking about the previous night. He couldn't wait to share the details. He knocked on his door and waited impatiently on the porch.

"Sonn." He called through the door as heard Razah approaching.

"Yo, be right out." Razah called back.

"Cool." A few seconds later Razah opened the door and they headed down the street.

Not wasting any time, Razah got right to the question at hand. "What happen last night kid?"

They say I couldn't play football, I was too small.
They say I couldn't play basketball, I wasn't tall,
They say I couldn't bag chicks at all.
Now Every Day of My Life I Ball!

"Yo! Dude, she put it on me fam." Mizz smiled.

"Say word, sonn." Razah said wanting details.

"Word. The pussy was so good, I made breakfast."

"Razah sonn, breakfast? You can't cook nigga."

"I was so fucked up B. I woulda fried some cereal kid." Razah laughed hard and loud. He then switched to a more serious tone. "Remember sonn, M.O.B."
Mizz looked at him. "Nigga, I just said the pussy was good. I'm on my G. Please believe dude, this ain't no love thing nigga, we just chillin'."

"One thing for sure my nigga, when that pussy start whipping fam, it's a muthafucker!" Razah pushed Mizz in the chest. "Worrrddd! But remember, you're a criminal mastermind not a lover, word!"

"I got you, sonn I got you."

While Mizz was recounting the night's events, Michaela was a having a leisurely morning in bed reliving the events herself. She couldn't get Mizz out of her mind. It had been better than she had expected and now she couldn't wait for it to happen again. She reached for the phone and called Tess to share her excitement.

"Hello, what's good? How was your weekend? " Tess answered, sounding like she had been up for awhile.

"Girl, guess what?" Michaela said excitedly.

"What girl?!" Tess knew her best friend had something juicy to tell her. "Oh, Sugar, what happened?"

"I saw him. Who? You know who!"

"Mizz, ooooooh shit! Mizz!"

"Lol! That nigga was chocolate and sexy. I was wit him! I was wit Big Mizz himself, but I was front'n being all shy and shit like I wasn't feeling him."

"Did he, did he?" The question hung in the air.

They say I couldn't play football, I was too small.
They say I couldn't play basketball, I wasn't tall,
They say I couldn't bag chicks at all.
Now Every Day of My Life I Ball!

Rather than answer, Michaela just laughed.

"You bitch, Wow! How was it?" Tess wanted details.

"It was like all I saw was fireworks and that sexy muthafucker made me breakfast." Her voice jumped.

"No, he didn't!" Tess couldn't believe what she was hearing.

"He surely did."

"What the hell?! Anyway, that's what's up. I wish I could find me a nigga like that shit! What about Marcus?"

"He drank too much, priorities was fucked up, couldn't help him. I know, fuck, I didn't want it to happen but it did. I had no control. Me and Marcus are done." Michaela thought for a moment about what she had thought was a good thing before things got bad and before she met Mizz.

"Yea, he was a loser. I loved him, but he still wanted to drink get passed out and do dumb shit. He put his alcohol before me, and all I did was try to help him. He was too old to be doing that dumb shit. He finished college and still lived at home with his parents at twenty six years old, come on! He'll never change! That's why I had to move on. But he will realize, I hope, someday and get his shit together. You don't know a good thing till it's gone."

"Hey girl, I know it hurts. Just focus on Mizz now. I'll call you later after school girl. And I'm glad you let Marcus go." Tess said offering her thoughts on the matter. Tess hung up and looked at the phone in disbelief. That certainly was not what she expected when she had picked up the phone.

They say I couldn't play football, I was too small.
They say I couldn't play basketball, I wasn't tall,
They say I couldn't bag chicks at all.
Now Every Day of My Life I Ball!

Heat Around the Corner

The inside of the police station buzzed with activity. Officers and detectives, all holding a cup of coffee in one hand and a cell phone in another, maneuvered their way around each other as if walking their assigned routes through the station. Newly arrested perps sat waiting for their turn to be processed and moved downstairs to the holding cells.

The major's face contorted into an even angrier shape than usual. He looked at his lieutenant and, not wanting any misunderstanding as to what he wanted and when he wanted it yelled, "By tomorrow, I want all this information on my fuckin desk. Don't let me down! What the fuck, mothafuckas!" He walked out of the lieutenant's office and slammed the door.

"Damn fuck!" the lieutenant's mouth hung open.

"Major is pissed, huh?" the young detective was known for his mastery of stating the obvious.

"He should be. Some muthafucker leaked some information about some shit to the Chief and he had no answers."

"About what, Lieutenant?"

"Leak Martin."

"Who the fuck is Leak Martin?"

"He is the cuzin of the high school star, Mizz."

"For real? That kid is nice!" the detective was a huge fan and had even been to the season opener.

"But let me tell you something that ain't nice." He got up and closed his door. "They saying Mizz and Razah, those high school kids, got something to do wit him and they're saying Mizz is the mastermind of the whole shit."

They say I couldn't play football, I was too small.
They say I couldn't play basketball, I wasn't tall,
They say I couldn't bag chicks at all.
Now Every Day of My Life I Ball!

"You gotta be kidding! Wait! Mastermind of what?"

"According to Major, he has the High Rises, the Terrace mostly."

"Sounds like bullshit." The detective said hardly believing what he was hearing.

"Maybe, but Major was pissed and wants a file in three days." The lieutenant answered.

"But what I'm wondering is why he would think those kids have something to do wit it, and Mizz the Mastermind?"

"No clue. Check it out. Let's get back to work."

Monday rolled around and Michaela was back at her school. While at lunch, she picked up the paper and was reading an article on Mizz when a boy she had never seen before came over and introduced himself.

"Hi, I'm Petey. Excuse me. Can I see that paper? That kid is great and the next NBA player."
She smiled. "Do you know him?" he asked her.

"Yea, you can see the paper no problem. And yes, I know him. And I'm Michaela, by the way."
Petey's heart beat quickened knowing that this could be the break he was looking for in the Leak Martin case. He had been placed there undercover to see if he could get any information or find someone with a connection to either Leak or Mizz.

"Do you think he can sign an autograph for me?" he asked trying to find out exactly how well she knew him.

"Sure, I don't see why not. Aren't you a new student in my Math class?" she asked.

"Yea, I'm new here."

"I'll tell you what. He just gave me tickets for the

They say I couldn't play football, I was too small.
They say I couldn't play basketball, I wasn't tall,
They say I couldn't bag chicks at all.
Now Every Day of My Life I Ball!

next game and its here at our school for the Christmas tournament."

"Those tickets been sold out."

"I have three tickets. You can come with me and my girl, Chantress."

"Oh, my god! You're the best!" he said trying to contain his excitement but failing miserably.

"I'll talk to you more about it during last period." Michaela said hearing the bell and getting up from the table.

"Ok. Cool. Thanks so much."

After the last period ended, Michaela saw Petey hanging out in the café. She headed over and told him to meet her there before the game. "Hey Petey! Here's the deal, meet us here." She said pointing to a spot near the courts where the game would be held. Again not trying to sound too excited, and failing, he blurted "Hell yeah!! Anything!"

A couple of weeks later Petey eagerly waited for them at the agreed upon spot. He watched as the crowds made their way into the school. Just as he looked at his watch thinking that he might have been stood up, Michaela and Tess arrived with Leak and his crew not far behind.

"What's good girl, how you been? I haven't seen you in a minute." Leak said looking at Michaela.

"I'm good, just school and working. Nothing much."

"Hi, I'm Tess. Michaela is rude! Psych, just kidding." Tess said stepping in front of her friend.

"I'm Leak. What's up. And who's your boy?" he looked hard at Petey.

"What's up Bro? How are you? I'm Petey." Pete's voice cracked.

They say I couldn't play football, I was too small.
They say I couldn't play basketball, I wasn't tall,
They say I couldn't bag chicks at all.
Now Every Day of My Life I Ball!

"So Chantree and Petey, you friends with Mizz?" he asked with a hint of suspicion in his voice.

"I know Michaela from school." Petey answered.

"Michaela is my best friend." Tess added.

"She is good people." Leak said smiling at Michaela.

"What brings you here?" Tess asked.

"Mizz is family. I do anything for him. I mean anything." He said emphasizing the word anything.

"Wow, you guys must be close?!

"I said I will do anything. I practically raised him, but anyways enjoy the game." Leak and his crew said goodbye and made their way into the gym.

Petey sat down next to Tess and tried to piece together the connections that Michaela had with Mizz and Leak. He liked that he was getting close but still had to get a hell of a lot closer.

Razah found Leak and his crew and sat down to chat for awhile. He wanted to make sure that there wouldn't be a repeat performance of what had happened at the opening game. Feeling like he had made himself clear, he went over to see Michaela and Tess.

"Damn, you girls are definitely the finest chicks in here! Shit!" he said being his typical charming self.

"Who's your boy?"

"What's up my dude? You chillin?" Petey raised his hand in a half-wave.

"The question is who you here wit, dude?" Razah said cool like as he looked at him.

"It's not like that. We all friends. I just came to see the game, Homie."

"Ok, cool. No disrespect. Just wasn't trying to step over your toes cuz I'm about to bag Tess. Feel me my

They say I couldn't play football, I was too small.
They say I couldn't play basketball, I wasn't tall,
They say I couldn't bag chicks at all.
Now Every Day of My Life I Ball!

dude?" Razah said laughing trying to lighten the mood.

"I got you!" Petey laughed too.

"You crazy nigga!" Tess said hitting Razah's arm.

"Razah, you going to sit wit us?" Michaela asked.

"Nah, I'm going to sit with the fam tonight and talk business."

"Business? What business your ignorant ass got?!" Razah rolled his eyes. "Holla at me, girl!" he said looking at Tess.

"Ok, whatever you say boy! I'll call you if you lucky!" she laughed.

Razah walked off and headed back across the stands to discuss business with Leak and the crew. He dapped the crew and leaned in whispering something in Leak's ear. Leak nodded, whispered back and called Michaela over.

"Hey, after the game we going to chill at the crib. If you wanna, come chill, you and your friends. " Razah said.

"Ok, Cool. I'll hit you up." She said smiling. Cool."

The game started and Mizz continued with his usual routine leaving players in his dust as he hit shot after shot. He was fouled and went to the line for a couple of free throws. Just before he took his first shot, he scanned the crowd looking for Razah and Michaela. He found them and to his surprise, sitting next to them is his crew, Tess and someone he had never seen before. 'Who the fuck is that,' he thought to himself as he drained the second foul shout. He then called a timeout. Razah caught his drift and made his way to the seats behind the bench.

"Who the fuck is that bird ass nigga wit Michaela and them?" Mizz asked.

"Some nut ass nigga from school," Razah replied.

They say I couldn't play football, I was too small.
They say I couldn't play basketball, I wasn't tall,
They say I couldn't bag chicks at all.
Now Every Day of My Life I Ball!

"Word B! I don't trust him." Mizz hoped he was making his point.

"Ok. Word son!" Razah replied, understanding perfectly and agreeing completely.

Michaela looked at them wondering what they could be talking about in the middle of the game. "Did you see that?" She asked Tess.

"That was weird. They both looked over here and started talking. Them two are wild. They seem up to something." Tess answered letting the word 'something' hang in the air for a minute.

"Yea, that was weird." Petey said. "Like they saw something that they didn't like."

The game ended and Mizz had yet another stellar finish with forty-three points, nine assists, and eight rebounds. Mizz and Razah stood around after the game discussing Petey and making gestures to Leak and his crew. Mizz looked up at Michaela and signaled that he would call her later. They bumped fists and Mizz headed into the locker room while Razah went and talked with the crew.

"Ladies and gents, sorry tonight won't be good. Maybe next time." He said.

"Oh, sugar! I wanted to chill." Michaela was genuinely disappointed.

"Me too. Damn, oh well. I guess we can get up another time." Tess said.

"For sure, Homies for sure. I'll tell Mizz to holla at you M-Easy." He said smiling at Michaela.

"Ok, Sweetie." Michaela and Tess said goodbye and headed out. Petey followed right behind wondering when he would get another chance to hang with Mizz and his friends.

They say I couldn't play football, I was too small.
They say I couldn't play basketball, I wasn't tall,
They say I couldn't bag chicks at all.
Now Every Day of My Life I Ball!

The next day Petey waited outside the lieutenant's office thinking about his next move. The lieutenant hung up the phone and called him in to sit down.

"Lieutenant, we need to talk, sir. It's very important." Petey said.

"Ok. Give me ten minutes, alright?" the lieutenant did not want to waste time if all Petey had to offer turned out to be nothing but smoke.

"Ok." Petey agreed.

"Ok, go ahead."

"Remember the dude, Leak?"

"Of course I remember that asshole."

"I never stopped following that clown. I believe I'm on to something. I'm doing my usual undercover duties at the high school and I saw that high school kid star in the paper.

"And, so what?"

"Anyways, this girl he talks to had tickets to the game so I went. And at the game, guess who she was friends wit?" Petey asked trying to build up drama.

"Leak, so what? That means nothing."

"Razah invited us out to chill out wit Leak and them but I then saw Razah whisper something to Mizz in his ear. He then looked at us. At the end of the game, Razah came back and said it wasn't going to happen. It was so weird so we didn't end up going." This time Petey got his attention.

The lieutenant nodded, "Yeah, that's something. Wow! See what else you could find out. Good work, Petey. I would love to butt fuck that bastard for real."

"Peep this though, what I found out. The Leak kid is the cousin of that phenomenon Mizzier, the high school genius and his sidekick Myshawn "aka" Razah. They are everywhere. The word on the street is that Leak has five of

They say I couldn't play football, I was too small.
They say I couldn't play basketball, I wasn't tall,
They say I couldn't bag chicks at all.
Now Every Day of My Life I Ball!

the seven towers in the terrace. That's ten stairwells in five high rises, not counting the low rises and the corners. That's theirs, too. The word is that Mizz is the mastermind behind the whole thing."

The lieutenant leaned in to concentrate on what Petey was saying because if what his gut was telling him was right, he had stumbled onto something huge. "You can't be serious." He said.

"And at every basketball game he is there scaring anyone that attempts to even look wrong at that kid Mizz. Him and the rest of his crew: Jack, Murtock, Rondo, and a beautiful girl named Sority. I saw them at the game, and the more and more I see those two crooks, I feel like they have something to do wit them. Leak is the cousin of Mizz, so I believe Mizz is, in fact, the mastermind."

"Damn, if that is true. This would be a war on drugs." The lieutenant said, stunned.

"Mizz and Razah are the new power. Not only in their sports; I'm telling you on the streets, too. But you can't even call this shit a war." Petey said as he stood up and walked around the office.

"Why not?"

"Because wars end!" Petey said pounding his fist on the lieutenant's desk.

"Here is a true fact, but no one says if you follow the drugs you got a drug case, you follow the money you don't know where you end up." The lieutenant stated, walked over to the door, opened it and told Petey to stop wasting time and get his ass back to work.

They say I couldn't play football, I was too small.
They say I couldn't play basketball, I wasn't tall,
They say I couldn't bag chicks at all.
Now Every Day of My Life I Ball!

Loyalty is Key

Later on that evening, Mizz called a meeting and sent Razah to gather the troops to join him at the abandoned spot. An hour later Mizz stood and addressed his crew.

"How's everyone doing? I don't have to ask, I see shit, niggas." He looked around at each of the members. Some were dressed just a little too nice and wore just a little too much bling for his comfort. He continued, lowering his voice so that they had to focus on what he was saying. "Remember, be careful wit your purchases. Now, let's get down to business. I just want to reinforce something cuz we not slipping. I just want us to remember we family and loyalty is the key.

Loyalty, this part of the game you got your peoples. If you don't have family in this world what do you have, muthafuckers. My niggas, we gotta run a tight ship out here. You feel me? You don't hand no money to no one that matters and don't take no product from no one that matters. If you do any of this nonsense, you done bumped your mothafuckin head and we all are done. So until we meet again, niggas. May all your jumps hit nothing but the bottom of the net." He signed to the crew and he and Razah left.

Mizz sat in his room after the meeting thinking about everything but mostly about Michaela. He decided to call her to find out who he had seen her with at the game.

"Hello, Michaela."

"Hey boy, what's up I see you been killing?"

"Yea girl you know how I do?" he got right down to business. "Quick question? I peeped ya at the game the

They say I couldn't play football, I was too small.
They say I couldn't play basketball, I wasn't tall,
They say I couldn't bag chicks at all.
Now Every Day of My Life I Ball!

other night looking dumb good as always but who was the nigga you was wit though?"

"Petey, he is in my class at school?" she said wondering why he was so interested.

"Really? I never heard you speak about him before. What's good wit that nigga?"

"He is harmless he came up to me one day, I was looking at the newspaper and he said he was your biggest fan."

"Word, ightta hahahah just like that huh?"

"Yea, just like that that, dude was sweating you real hard too like you important or something.
So I had another ticket for the game, my aunt didn't want to come cuz she was busy so I said he could come."

"So that is how it went down huh? No butt licking." She laughed. "You are the funniest dude I know, you have nothing to worry about."

"You straight, we straight I was just trying holla at you and see what was good, mommy I will holla in the a.m. sexy girl."

"Ok, Mike Air Jordan. Sleep tight." She said kissing him through the phone.

"You too." He said and kissed back.

As soon as he hung up, he picked up a second phone they used only for business and called Razah.

"Sonn, get b, we might have a problem for real my nigga." Mizz said without saying hello.

"What's good? " he continued, "Remember the nigga that was at the game wit Michaela, and Tess?"

"Yea, what up B?" Razah asked wondering what he was saying.

"Watch that nigga he might be a pig, he look like

They say I couldn't play football, I was too small.
They say I couldn't play basketball, I wasn't tall,
They say I couldn't bag chicks at all.
Now Every Day of My Life I Ball!

one."

"Ewhhhhhh!!!!! Word sonn how you figure b?"

He was in no mood to argue. "Just watch him, he look corny sonn word. You see his face sonn? It's corny b. Just watch him especially the way Michaela said he was sweating me like flies to shit, and the way she met him. Plus I wanna see how the nigga play and see if he reacts wit anyone in the crew feel me?"

"No doubt sonn, I'm on it b."

Things were pretty status quo as the Christmas break finally arrived. Business was booming and Leak decided to throw Mizz a little birthday party at his new club. He had opened it only a few months ago and had decided to call it, "Just Us," in respect to the family.

Mizz walked into the club not expecting to see everyone there, especially Michaela and Tess. They all wished him happy birthday. He made his way around saying "hi" and "thank you" to everyone. He then called the family together for a little meeting upstairs in Leak's office which was actually Mizz's office.

"A new American dream, anything can be accomplished as long as you are loyal to those who are loyal to you. Don't forget where you come from and where you are going! This is hard work, this what you get, I wanna get a toast to my family to death do us part. Keep the motto Mob." He raised a glass to each of them. He signed to the crew and went downstairs to rejoin the party.

Later on that night, he pulled Razah aside. "One of the reasons for our success is you. We're probably the smartest sixteen year olds in the world. Let's keep it that way, we work too hard to go out like Alpo and Rich Porter over some B.S. you feel me, we gotta hold each other

They say I couldn't play football, I was too small.
They say I couldn't play basketball, I wasn't tall,
They say I couldn't bag chicks at all.
Now Every Day of My Life I Ball!

down. When its time to get, we will walk away on top. Believe me, on top," Mizz emphasized by raising his hand as high as he could like it was a jump shot, "none of the fuk shit. Cuz me, we," he said gestering to Razah and back to himself, "we gonna do things the right way. Failing is not an option. Razah, brotha, it's not all about success. It's also about survival and loyalty. You remember the Michael Jordan commercial 'I fail over and over again that's why I succeed'? Nothing and no one will come between you and me. I love you man." He hugged Razah tightly.

"I love you too." Razah said hugging him back.
Petey had heard about the party from Michaela and Tess and had decided to try his luck at crashing it. He stood outside the club and knocked hoping someone would hear. Leak looked out the door and saw that it was Petey. He told Mizz then waited for instructions. Mizz gave the okay to let him in. Petey stepped inside the club not knowing what to expect. Mizz just looked at him.

"Although we have never met I just wanted to say happy b day. I'm good friends wit Michaela."

"Yo name is what bro?" Mizz asked.
Petey ignored the question and continued. "And I'm a fan of yours too, bro."

"Ok well enjoy yourself." Mizz said pointing to the food and other refreshments.

Petey mingled while he scoped out everything and everyone looking to see if there was anyone that might not be family and that might fold under pressure. He made mental notes of several potential targets.

Mizz and Razah hung back in a corner and watched his every move, especially his move to leave only twenty minutes after he arrived. They both looked at each other,

They say I couldn't play football, I was too small.
They say I couldn't play basketball, I wasn't tall,
They say I couldn't bag chicks at all.
Now Every Day of My Life I Ball!

knowing what the other was thinking. Deciding to keep shit under wraps until later, they rejoined the party.

The next day at the station, Petey stood at the bulletin board in front of the lieutenant and the other detectives. He wrote a bunch of names down and circled several.

"You guys won't believe what I came up wit, it's amazing but this is how I see it." Petey started.

"Ok. Go ahead. Let me what you come up with or whatever you propose." The lieutenant said.

Petey looked at the other detectives and took a deep breath before starting to lay everything out. "Does the name Mizzier ring a bell? Or should I say Mizz? He was born in Waterbury, Connecticut. He is the number one ranked basketball player in the country and also the number one ranked student-athlete in the world with a 4.0 GPA. His crew consists of five people which are all family and the rest are workers. His right hand man is Myshawn aka Razah," he said letting the detectives make the connection in their minds. "He is the number one football player in the country and the number two student-athlete in the world, also with a 4.0 GPA right behind Mizz. Both are only sixteen years old, unbelievable. He then wrote three names on the board behind him and pointed to them in succession before continuing. "Leak is the cousin of Mizz and has been in the game hustling for years. Murdock is the hit man and muscle. Chantress is the runner and get this, also a model for Segue Inc.

Mizz seems to be an ordinary kid but you will only ever see him at his basketball games. He's like Mr. Untouchable. I have been following this kid for a minute and make no mistake he is still a kid; he gets up and he and his neighbor Razah walk to school every day, and after

They say I couldn't play football, I was too small.
They say I couldn't play basketball, I wasn't tall,
They say I couldn't bag chicks at all.
Now Every Day of My Life I Ball!

school he goes to b ball practice. Then after practice he walks home with no contact with anyone. He is a very low key kid and doesn't draw any attention to himself." The detectives looked at him and then each other shaking their heads. The lieutenant spoke, knowing that he was not alone in his thinking.

"Damn are you sure Petey? Shiiitt, this ain't your particular house old lil' nigga hustling drugs."

"Nah, but don't forget Marcus Robinson was low key and ran this city for years."

The Lieutenant thought for a moment. "So what you're saying is, this kid Mizzier replaced Marc Rob and he is the new kingpin of these parts? Petey are you smoking dust? That sounds crazy, better yet nutty." Petey ignored the comment and continued.

"Everything he does is like Marcus and who is a better teacher than the one you looked up too. They moved five hundred to a thousand keys of this shit as a family. In fact, they sold more than a ton of this bullshit. That equals seventy to ninety people on both sides of the street. It's like the 1st and 15th of every month but it was every day. This young nigga got this set up like a fortune 500 company. He got niggas punching a clock for all shifts, even overtime. You had the option of morning shifts 7am-3pm, second shift 3pm-11pm, then graveyard 11pm-7am. These mothafuckas were selling like nine to ten keys a day. Mizz has a tremendous intellect and the leadership skills to build an empire bigger than Nino Brown. He is like Scarface. We have never seen anything like this before in our time. This dude is doing what a lot of old timers are scared to do. Two hundred keys a week but with the epidemic of crack and cocaine. These muthafuckers, with whatever they're

They say I couldn't play football, I was too small.
They say I couldn't play basketball, I wasn't tall,
They say I couldn't bag chicks at all.
Now Every Day of My Life I Ball!

selling, are moving up to two thousand keys a week with gross profit up to seventy million dollars. It's estimated that these young masterminds are bringing in thirty million a month."

Petey cleared his throat. "It's not Mizz we are after. It's the supplier and who ever he is working for and the bastard that is bringing in this stuff.

Again the lieutenant thought before he spoke. He wanted to make sure he chose his words carefully. "Ok, so what do you have besides instincts that will hold any weight in court? Cuz let me tell you, this is nothing. This shit sure ain't going to do the job. Without the drugs and informants none of these scum bags muthafuckers are going to jail, Petey. We will just be wasting our time and a lot of police work." He hoped that he had made himself crystal clear.

"And we ain't going to get no informants in that family that's for sure."

Wanting to be more cautious and avoid any potential problems, Mizz went over some new ideas in his mind as he waited to hook up with Razah. Since this had truly become a business and not just your standard drug deal operation, course it was also no standard drug, he also wanted things to be more efficient. How to achieve that was a different story. Eager to share his ideas, he met up with Razah and they headed off to school.

"Yo, Razah, we need to build an exact replica of the drug labs sonn."

"Why sonn?" asked Razah, a little puzzled at the suggestion.

"Just trust me sonn."

"Ok fam." Razah shrugged. "Anyway bro, you got a big game nigga word b this week."

They say I couldn't play football, I was too small.
They say I couldn't play basketball, I wasn't tall,
They say I couldn't bag chicks at all.
Now Every Day of My Life I Ball!

"Hell yeah, Sonn! A couple more games before the state tournament. Sonn, word. Plus too, sonn, it's something dumb important I'm forgetting. Dooke word."

"Nigga, we another convention my dude, damn." Razah said remembering.

"You fucking right kid, all this other shit is on my mind. Mizz sighed. "Sonn, especially the other night that Petey shit. Sonn word, I'm going to get Tess on her B, with her fine ass to see what's good wit the nigga."

"Tess!" Razah looked at Mizz. "Worrrddd, sonn. Damn, B I wanted to hit that fam."

Mizz laughed. "Take one for the team bro; pussy is a powerful thing my nigga. Stop being a sambo, ighttttaaahh, and the bitch is dumb bad B."

"Yea, you right. I don't trust that fag uncle tom nigga anyway, sonn. Something ain't right with that bitch, my nigga." Razah agreed but was still disappointed that he wouldn't be able to play.

"I haven't pin-pointed it yet, sonn, but trust B I will my nigga, feel me. But, I will call Michaela and tell her what's good, nigga. Smell me."

"No doubt sonn, word." Razah said, nodding his head.

"I gotta holla at coach. Holla back sonn!" They dapped each other up and Mizz headed off to see his coach. He hadn't talk to him since the Christmas holiday breaks, so he went to check with him to see what was good.

"Mizz how was your Christmas break?" the coach asked. "How's your family?"

"I'm Muslim coach so I don't celebrate Christmas but if someone gives me a gift I will sure take it." Mizz laughed. "The good thing is it was a week off, so I enjoyed it." You're a funny dude, Mizz. On a serious note we only

They say I couldn't play football, I was too small.
They say I couldn't play basketball, I wasn't tall,
They say I couldn't bag chicks at all.
Now Every Day of My Life I Ball!

have a few games before the state tournament starts. Mizz, it's our time this year," the coach put his hand on Mizz's shoulder. And if we are going to get a chip, it's this season. We're good at every position."

"Coach, me too; everyone is working hard and I'm staying focused thanks to Allah, the man upstairs." Mizz pointed to the ceiling.

"This is good. Always good to give praises to Allah no matter if I have a different religion from you. Always acknowledge the man upstairs. And you will be blessed and successful, thinking and feeling that way. That is so true that nothing can be done without faith in God." Coach also pointed toward the ceiling. "Just let me know the colleges that are in your main interest cuz they are overwhelmingly hitting me up. The funny thing, a few asked me about a package deal wit you and your boy, Razah!"

"Word! Ightahhhhhhhhh." Mizz liked the sound of that.

'What's that mean, anyway?' Coach scratched his head and wished he had an interpreter sometimes. "But Mizz, my whole reason for talking to you is that to make sure you stay focused bro."

"Thanks Coach." Mizz looked his coach directly in the eyes. "I will not let the team or myself down, and especially not you cuz I know all the trust that you have in me." Mizz thought for a moment what his coach or his team would do if they knew about the operation. He said goodbye and left the locker room. On the way out of school, he called Michaela to talk to her about hooking Tess up with Petey. He figured this was the best way to keep tabs on him since he didn't trust him or know his true story was.

They say I couldn't play football, I was too small.
They say I couldn't play basketball, I wasn't tall,
They say I couldn't bag chicks at all.
Now Every Day of My Life I Ball!

"Hello." Michaela answered in her usual sweet voice.

"Hey sexy girl." Mizz responded in his.

"Hey stranger, where you been hiding?"

"I've been chilling, staying focused, and trying to make the tournament and shit. The season is almost done."

"Ok, I understand." She did understand but still felt a little neglected. "So what's on your mind babe?"

He got right down to business. "Babe what's really good wit that nigga Petey? I'm not feeling this nigga. For real, something ain't right wit him. Just look at him. Look at his face. He's corny!"

She laughed. "He's straight, he's cute. But Mizz you right, he is corny. Why don't you trust him though?"

Mizz sighed. "He just seems corky and shit and a snake two-face dick rider. Do me a favor. Put Tess on him so she can feel the nigga out, then I can see what's really good."

"Excuse me what?" She wasn't sure she heard him right. At least, she hoped she didn't. "Hook Tess up wit him for real?"

"Tess is fly. She got a big ass, nice tits. She's perfect 9-10. Everybody want a relationship wit her. The last nigga she fucked wit, after she walked out on the nigga, he ain't been the same. I still see that nut ass nigga crying and shit, wanting her back to no end. I know she is the answer for luring in this clown nigga. No doubt." He hoped he was getting through to her.

"Ok, what actually do you want her to do? Luring him in for what?"

"Just make sure he wants to be closer to her and he trusts her completely. The more time they spend together, the better for us and the information we can obtain"

Mizz couldn't see her through the phone, but Michaela put

They say I couldn't play football, I was too small.
They say I couldn't play basketball, I wasn't tall,
They say I couldn't bag chicks at all.
Now Every Day of My Life I Ball!

the phone at arm's length and shook her head before she responded to his request. "Mizz, that's kind of fucked up. I just thought you wanted her to chill and hangout wit him, not lead him on and then infiltrate and especially break his heart. She doesn't have the type of training for that."

"Damn! My bad, no disrespect intended. Let's be real. What the fuck you mean lie to him and bullshit the nigga. Are you serious? She a bitch, shit she got all the training she needs." Mizz didn't hold back having had his heart broken a few times himself.

"Ooooooh." She liked Mizz, but sometimes he surprised her with shit that she didn't like. "Mizz, your mouth is so nasty at times. All rightttty then. You a mess nigga, ok! But I'm telling you he is straight." She sighed.

"You my baby and Tess will do anything for you."

"Thanks babe." Mizz relaxed his tone with her. "I will look forward to seeing and chilling wit you at the end of the month at the convention."

"Yes, anytime to chill wit you I look forward to as well, baby."

"Cool, gotta jet. I will hit you later beautiful 100." Mizz had accomplished exactly what he had set out to do.

"Bye babe." She hung up the phone wondering what the conversation had really been about. She decided that she would get the scoop at some point, but for now she had to run this idea by Tess, who she knew would do anything for her. She picked up the phone and dialed her best friend.

"Hello." Tess answered.

"Hey girl, what's going?" She saw no point in waiting, so she came right out with it. "Listen I just got off the phone wit Mizz."

"Really, what that negro talking 'bout?"

They say I couldn't play football, I was too small.
They say I couldn't play basketball, I wasn't tall,
They say I couldn't bag chicks at all.
Now Every Day of My Life I Ball!

"This nigga said he don't trust Petey."

"Don't trust Petey, why? That's weird he's so innocent and sweet."

"Yesa, you know that crazy negro Mizz is always coming up wit something. He believes the nigga is a snake, and he phony. The scary thing is the nigga never be wrong. His instinct is always on point."

"I know! I will do anything for Mizz; he is like a brother to me. Of course I will see what's good wit Petey. Not a problem."

"Thanks, luv you girl."

"Michaela, you know better than that, you my bitch" Tess laughed. "Bye baby."

"Okay, bye." Michaela said, smiling. As soon as she got off the phone, she texted Mizz letting him know that Tess was down and she had his back. Mizz read the text and thought to himself 'Word, no doubt.'

They say I couldn't play football, I was too small.
They say I couldn't play basketball, I wasn't tall,
They say I couldn't bag chicks at all.
Now Every Day of My Life I Ball!

A Dude Will do Anything for Some ...

A week later, Mizz met up with Razah before his game to discuss business and the Petey situation. "Sonn, what's poppin wit the replica of the drug lab?' Mizz asked hoping to hear that it was about finished.

"Done, sonn!" Razah proudly said.

"Ightahhhhhhhhhhhhhh!" Mizz was thrilled. "Yo, I was wondering if Michaela was coming to the game tonight, sonn, wit Tess and that fuck nigga B?"

"You haven't even spoken to them niggas, sonn?" Razah was shocked.

"Nah, been mad busy. What up wit Leak and everyone sonn? Word."

"You know they will be in the building my nigga, ightaaaaah." Razah said.

"Iaght, word. Yo sonn, Tess fucking that nigga mad good B. He's probably all lovey dovey wit that bitch B, word. Then the dumb ass nigga telling her everything underneath the sun." Mizz thought about Petey getting played and smiled.

"Hell yeah, sonn. She probably threw that cock on the bum ass nigga." Razah agreed.

"Yeah, he probably dumb open o nut ass nigga." Both Mizz and Razah laughed hard thinking about Petey.

"Yea, damn sonn, you talk them up there, they go right there, sonn look." Razah said thinking about Tess.

"I see them muthafuckers." Mizz said looking into the stands. "Let me hit these lay ups B. I will holla after the game, sonn." Mizz stepped onto the court and started warming up. As usual, he busted ass ending the game with forty points, seven assists, and nine rebounds. After the

They say I couldn't play football, I was too small.
They say I couldn't play basketball, I wasn't tall,
They say I couldn't bag chicks at all.
Now Every Day of My Life I Ball!

game Petey and Tess got to know each other better while Mizz and Razah peeped them out. Tess turned around and gave Mizz a knowing smile as she left the gym with Petey and headed out to the parking lot. Mizz and Razah dapped each other up and Mizz headed off to the locker room knowing that the situation was in good hands.
Petey and Tess stood at his car and chatted. "Hey what's good?" Petey opened his car door. "You want a ride to your crib?" he asked shyly.

"You don't have to bring me home." Tess said politely denying the offer. "I will catch a cab home, okay. Thanks for the offer, though."

"I see you didn't want to wait for Michaela so I feel it's a necessity. I don't mind." Petey countered not wanting to take no for an answer.

"Michaela's aunt is coming to get her. Plus she is waiting for Mizz, and I kinda do mind." She was getting a little annoyed.

"Damn you been wigging all night." Petey started to get defensive. "What the hell did I do to you?"

"Wigging what's that?" She rolled her eyes at the comment. "Anyway you didn't do nothing. I just wanna chill alone, iaght"

"Well, I'm not feeling that, so I'm going to be a bugga boo and walk wit you all the way to your crib." Petey wasn't ready to give up yet.
Tess smiled. "I think you should be going home. Anyways it's late and we got school tomorrow, plus heard your pops be tripping."

"That's my uncle. That nigga's crazy. I supposed to bring the whip back asap after the game.
Fuck it I'll chill now and suffer later." They started

They say I couldn't play football, I was too small.
They say I couldn't play basketball, I wasn't tall,
They say I couldn't bag chicks at all.
Now Every Day of My Life I Ball!

walking towards Tess's home.

"But being in trouble can last forever especially what they say about your peoples."

"That's a true story. Punishments can last a life time. I remember one time I got grounded for sneaking a chick in the crib. That nigga still talking 'bout that bullshit. For real, my uncle is cool but he just wants me to do the right thing."

"Michaela told me what happen wit your moms and pops."

"Yea, that's why I live wit my uncle. They were in a bad accident and they need special attention. Thanks, that was a minute ago." Petey said shrugging. "So much about me. By the way what your peoples do?"

"My dad owns a couple of 7-11's"

"Ooooooh. Damn, I know you niggas be getting it in crazy slurpees and shit."

Tess laughed. "And my mom use to work for Omni Care. Now she helps my dad run the business."

"I'm surprised you don't work there and help out."

"I really don't have time wit school and stuff. I wanna get ready for college"

Petey nodded. "So do I. I started going to official visits to colleges and filling out apps and stuff."

"Damn boy, you focused. Aren't those apps crazy? The ivy league schools are a mess." She said.

"Shit, that outta my league. You mad smart."

"Hold, let me see if my light is on." Tess said as they approached her house. She breathed a sigh of relief. "Shit, good I'm home before them."

"So what's good wit you and your girl? You two are the baddest tandem in school. I know you have dudes of all races in the palm of your hands." He noticed that she was

They say I couldn't play football, I was too small.
They say I couldn't play basketball, I wasn't tall,
They say I couldn't bag chicks at all.
Now Every Day of My Life I Ball!

smiling. "Anyway, on that note, I'm glad you let me walk you home tonight, Tess."

"You mad cool, too." She said remembering what Mizz had asked her to do.

Petey looked into her eyes and leaned in to kiss her. She backed away, avoiding his approach.

"Bro, ain't you feeling Michaela?" She asked.

"I was, but I don't know her like I know you now and she got a man." He said trying to recover from misreading the moment.

"Ok, cool," Tess said hoping he got the point and wouldn't try to kiss her again. "I will see you later then."

"Ok, fine beautiful." He said trying to save a little of his dignity. "I will see you tomorrow."

"Sorry, I would let you in but my people are on their way home. I would let you upstairs, Petey." She changed her tone remembering about Mizz. She was hoping that her earlier move didn't ruin her chances.

He was confused by this sudden change of attitude.

"It's not a problem, Tess. For real, it's straight."

Before he knew it Tess had taken him by the hand, up the stairs of her house and they were in her bedroom kissing, slobbering and dry humping on the bed. He went to unzip her pants when she sat up and sighed. "Hold on. Wait this ain't right.

Petey looked at her. "What you mean? You givin a nigga blue balls ain't right. You being a cock tease.

Tess got off the bed. "Word nigga!" she said raising her voice slightly. "Black mothafucka you was telling me fifteen minutes ago you was feelin' my girl, now you trying to fuck me." Petey put up his hands looking like he was surrendering. "Look baby, real talk. I don't want you doing

They say I couldn't play football, I was too small.
They say I couldn't play basketball, I wasn't tall,
They say I couldn't bag chicks at all.
Now Every Day of My Life I Ball!

nothing that you don't want to do. You want me to bounce? Fine."

"FUCK YOU whack ass nigga!" She yelled while buttoning her pants.

Petey, horny as hell was not ready to leave yet. He had to find a way to salvage this. "Hold on, mommy let's talk." He said trying to look deep into her eyes.

She scowled. "What is it that you want to talk about? Is it about what you want?"

"You serious right now. You buggin. Look sweetheart, both of you are extremely attractive and it seems like you want me to make a decision. You are who I want as a friend and if I felt anything is going to work we should be companions then we should be lovers. Now that is out the way, where were we?" Seeing an opportunity, he jumped back on Tess and started kissing her again. Tess gave in and asked if he had a condom.

"Hell yeah I got one." He said unable to hide his excitement.

Tess stopped him and looked. "Ok , damn! Is this regular for you? Are you always prepared like this?"

Barely hearing her, he pulled out a condom and tried to open it, but it got stuck to the wrapper.

Tess couldn't believe what she was seeing. "Nigga, hell no! That condom is old as hell; how long have you had that in your wallet?"Petey had enough. "Fuck, this is bullshit!" He said, thinking he's never gonna be able to get some at this rate.

"There will be other times." She said as she finished buttoning her shirt and straightening herself out.

"Shit, it will be a long time from now." He said disappointed that the moment had ended.

They say I couldn't play football, I was too small.
They say I couldn't play basketball, I wasn't tall,
They say I couldn't bag chicks at all.
Now Every Day of My Life I Ball!

They looked at each other when they heard a car pull up and the neighbor's dog barking. A beam of light shined into her room. Her parents were home. They had only moments before her parents would be inside.

Petey, still horny as hell, and now nervous as hell too, looked at Tess." Damn you sexy. What am I supposed to do now?"

"Get your dumb ass out nigga. My parents are home!" She said laughing out loud.

Her parents could be heard outside walking to the door and talking about the movie they had just seen.

"That movie was excellent. We need to get out more." Her mom said as they entered the house.

"Of course honey. I have just been so busy at work."

Petey threw on his shirt and tried to jump out the window. Tess told him how crazy he was and told him to take the side door. The neighbor's dog continued barking mad loud as Petey quickly jumped the fence and made his way out. Tess then climbed under the covers and pretended to be asleep as her parents checked on her. Fifteen minutes later, she picked up the phone and called Michaela to report back on the evening's events.

"Hello." Michaela answered sounding half-asleep.

"Bitch, I got something to tell you!" Tess couldn't wait to tell her what had happened.

"What happened?"

"Girl, that nigga sweating. Tell Mizz, we straight!"

"Ok, cool." She knew her friend would come through for her. "Damn, bitch that's wazzup. I will tell him

They say I couldn't play football, I was too small.
They say I couldn't play basketball, I wasn't tall,
They say I couldn't bag chicks at all.
Now Every Day of My Life I Ball!

in the morning cuz it is mad late right now. Bitch, tell me the rest in the morning I'm tired as hell."

"Ok , girl goodnight." Tess hung up the phone knowing that Mizz would be very happy when Michaela gave him the news. She rolled over and went to sleep thinking about her next move with Petey.

They say I couldn't play football, I was too small.
They say I couldn't play basketball, I wasn't tall,
They say I couldn't bag chicks at all.
Now Every Day of My Life I Ball!

You Can't Play a Playa

Early the next morning Michaela called Mizz to give him
the low down on what happened wit Petey and Tess. She
missed him and was excited to talk to him.

"Great game last night honey, very impressive. But
you cocky bastard, you already know that! No need to give
you a bigger head." She said half-joking.

"Thanks babe, but you only telling the truth." Mizz
laughed. "What's poppin wit the situation, sexy girl?"
"Babe, damn no I miss you, or how are you? You just right
to the point just like an insensitive negro." She was
annoyed that he seemed to just always be about business.
Michaela continued without waiting for Mizz to reply.

"Well, she's my girl; the bitch got the nigga right
where she wants him."

"Well, sexy girl, here is a true statement." Mizz said
sounding even more serious than usual. "We don't know
what we got, cuz we don't know what he got or his
intention for Tess or why he wants to chill wit us or her."

"Mizz, you so damn paranoid about everything, you
would think you were a drug dealer or something." She
said without thinking. "You scary all the time. "Loosen up
babe."

"Babe, I just don't trust people. Nothing is free,
everyone wants something. You know it's just all about
how they go about getting it." He backed off a little not
wanting to give her anymore ideas. "I just don't trust

They say I couldn't play football, I was too small.
They say I couldn't play basketball, I wasn't tall,
They say I couldn't bag chicks at all.
Now Every Day of My Life I Ball!

people. My bad."

"I guess you are right to some extent." Her voice softened. "Well, she did what you asked. She is in the nigga's realm now cuz he is feeling the bitch now."

"We just have to see how it plays out. Just like you if throw a nigga in a room wit a bunch a fags and he comes out wit a hard dick, that nigga that you thought was straight is guess what, a fucking fag. Patience is a virtue. People aren't what you think they are."

Michaela almost hung up the phone, but thought better against it. "Mizz, I can't stand you sometimes, you make me so sick. Aw, where do you come up wit these ignorant analogies? I'm getting off the phone. Talk to you later." She hung up without waiting to hear him say goodbye. She was starting to wonder about the true nature of Mizz and her relationship with him.

The next morning instead of going to school Petey headed to the station to tell the lieutenant about possible information on his new case and his new relationship with Tess. Tess, he thought, would lead him right to the inner circle or give him the information he needed without too much effort on his part. If he played his cards right, he would score that sweet ass in the process. He walked right into the lieutenant's office with a big shit-eating grin on his face.

"Good morning, Petey" The lieutenant was surprised to see him. "What brings you here to the office knowing that you suppose to be at school?"

"Hey, Lieutenant, chill out brotha." Petey said with sounding as cocky as he felt.

"No clown, you should have your black ass in school doing your fucking job. You sure as hell better have a good

They say I couldn't play football, I was too small.
They say I couldn't play basketball, I wasn't tall,
They say I couldn't bag chicks at all.
Now Every Day of My Life I Ball!

excuse why you here." He wasn't in the mood for any shit.
"Lieutenant, I chilled wit the best friend of Mizz's
girlfriend, Michaela. It was crazy and she is hot,
Lieutenant." He sounded like a boy who just saw his first
Playboy centerfold.

"Oh, really? Just cuz you probably got your piece
shined real good last night, she supposed to tell you
everything she knows about Mizz's scores and deals and
shit?" He couldn't believe he had to deal with this amateur.

"Petey, are you really in high school talking crazy like
this?"

"From her side of shit or mine, Lieutenant?" Petey sat
down and stretched. "No disrespect but it sounds like you
hating on a player."

"She wasn't exactly sweating you a month ago when
you met her." He decided he had to bring this love sick
puppy back to reality. "Did you forget you dealing wit a
genius? How you don't know Mizz ain't on to you? The
question is do you trust her?" Petey thought for a moment.

"It is funny, of course, wit the timing and all. Also wit
them clocking all the money, and drugs, the whole situation
is nothing that I'm not use to, but not ordinary though."
The lieutenant sighed thinking that maybe Petey wasn't
such a dumbass after all. "Well at least it came to your
mind what's going on." Petey leaned forward in his chair
starting to grasp the potential that Tess was just playing
him. "So what you're saying here, you don't believe a
damn word that she is saying, Lieutenant? Well, she can be
some spy of some sort, but I do think I can learn more from
her than she can from me."

"I see your point. I just hope you know what the fuck
you're doing, and you think wit the head on your shoulders

They say I couldn't play football, I was too small.
They say I couldn't play basketball, I wasn't tall,
They say I couldn't bag chicks at all.
Now Every Day of My Life I Ball!

and not your other one, Petey."

Petey's cockiness returned. "I'm just saying you sound like you don't want me to live, like you don't trust me or something, Lieutenant. Sorry if it's a dry well at your house and my faucet won't turn off. I don't know yet why the bitch is on me right now but rest assure I will find out. Good day lieutenant!" Petey slammed the door and walked out as he heard the lieutenant yelling behind him that he had one chance. He headed home to prepare for his date with Tess that night. He would show the lieutenant who was the smart one. In fact, he thought, maybe he would be lieutenant after he busted this case wide open.

Tess arrived at the museum just a few minutes before she had told Petey to meet her. She felt good about the way she looked and knew that he would be sweating her big time when he saw her in the nice tight black mini-skirt and low-cut blouse she had chosen. She felt good about her progress so far and figured that she would all but seal the deal that night. Just as she took out her phone to check the time, he touched her shoulder.

"Hey, what's up Tess? What's good wit you sweetheart?" he said as she turned around.

"Hey, Peter. How are you since we last saw each other?"

"Call me Petey. No one calls me Peter." He said remembering the torture he endured in a school thanks to a name synonymous for a part of the male anatomy.

Tess laughed, "No one accept me nigga. I call you Peter. You know why? Cuz I can." She said as she touched his arm.

"Wow, bust I see. I love a chick that keeps it funky."

"I do and always have."

They say I couldn't play football, I was too small.
They say I couldn't play basketball, I wasn't tall,
They say I couldn't bag chicks at all.
Now Every Day of My Life I Ball!

"My girlfriend is the same way," Petey blurted out without thinking. Tess looked stunned. "Well Peter, good for that bitch. You're a dick head. I didn't know you had a girlfriend, leading me on to thinking something else. You tried to play me and fuck me. You asshole!"

"Nah, ma be easy." He held up his hands. "Hold up, I see someone I know." He walked away to go chat with someone he knew from the force. Tess just stood there talking to herself about how this bum ass nigga trying to play her like he all fly or something.

Petey walked up to his friend, thankful for a minute to think about how to correct his little error. "Hey Sam, what's up guy? What are you doing here buddy?"

"Damn Petey, who is the hot chick? Yo dude. Damn she fine." Sam couldn't help but stare.

"It's the chick from the case that I'm working on."

"Oh really, I heard about the big bust you guys trying to create. But, who is the chick Petey? Damn." Sam was not exactly what one would call a lady's man and when he saw someone as hot as Tess, he just couldn't help himself.

"She is the best friend of the alleged suspect's girlfriend. She is bad alright."

"Fuck yea, I will sell my soul to the devil to get some of that pussy."

Petey laughed. "You mad funny." Changing his tone, he said, "I just told her I have a chick, though."

"Why in fuck's name would you do some dumb shit like that?"

Knowing he had made a mistake but wanting Sam to think otherwise, Petey said, "Relax my dude. No woman wants a man that another woman doesn't already have. Trust me." Sam shook his head. "Ok whatever, dude. Have

They say I couldn't play football, I was too small.
They say I couldn't play basketball, I wasn't tall,
They say I couldn't bag chicks at all.
Now Every Day of My Life I Ball!

a goodnight. See you at the station."

"Same to you Sam. Have a good one."

As Petey walked back to the entrance, Tess sat there pissed off and ready for the night to end. She did, however, consider letting the night continue just long enough to get a free meal off this clown and turn it into a little game of who plays who. She took a deep breath as he sat down.

"Sorry about that. He is an old neighbor of mine. Had to say 'hi'." He looked at her choosing his next words carefully. "Boy, you look extra stunning tonight."

She swallowed. "Thanks. You look ok and neat."

He smiled. "Thanks beautiful."

Struggling between wanting to get away for this lame ass corny nigga and keeping her word to Michaela, Tess continued to walk around the museum contemplating her next move. They came to a piece of art that they both appreciated.

"Damn this stuff is amazing and wild shit," Petey said standing just a little too close for Tess's comfort.

"Some people think that this stuff isn't ordinary. So basically, they don't understand it. But it's our culture," she replied, taking a step closer to the exhibit and a step further from him.

"Wow this is awesome, very unusual," Petey said walking up to another exhibit.

"That's an elephant tusk," Tess said sounding annoyed.

"That's weird I didn't know that Africans were in to baseball?"

"What? No it's elephant tusk. Yea, Yea," She said not sure what he was saying.

"I know. It was a joke." He explained.

"Please, that was dumb corny, Peter." She was feeling

They say I couldn't play football, I was too small.
They say I couldn't play basketball, I wasn't tall,
They say I couldn't bag chicks at all.
Now Every Day of My Life I Ball!

this clown less and less as the night continued, if that was possible. Finally they sat down to eat.

"I come here quite often to clear my head," Petey said picking up the menu. "The Shrimp Alfredo is the best on the menu as far as I'm concerned, but get whatever you want."

"I'm sorry, what were you saying?" Tess said distracted by her overwhelming desire to not be there anymore.

"I was saying I eat here a lot and I know you can't stop thinking about me."

She was reaching her breaking point. "Again, Peter my bad. I'm not focused right now my mind is elsewhere. Did you just say I can't stop thinking about you? Never mind, can we just order the food?"

The waitress comes over and takes their order. "How are you? I will have the Shrimp Alfredo," Petey said, trying to sound smooth.

"No, not today clown," Tess interrupted and asked the waitress to come back later.

"Ok baby, whatever you say. Let me ask you something why do you think I'm so hot?"

She couldn't believe she was sitting across from such an idiot. She had had enough. "Only thing that is hot about you is your breath. For real, Peter." He put his hand up to his mouth, breathed into it and took a whiff. "Damn you can smell that shit? I suppose to get my tooth fixed. They bullshitting on the insurance." He hoped she hadn't heard that last part. "Dammmnnn, they better hurry up before your tongue fall out your mouth." She said covering her nose. Petey stood up. "Sorry, I'm going to the bathroom to wash my hands. Don't miss me too much."

They say I couldn't play football, I was too small.
They say I couldn't play basketball, I wasn't tall,
They say I couldn't bag chicks at all,
Now Every Day of My Life I Ball!

"Ok, don't forget to brush the shit on your tongue." She said laughing. "Can you get the waitress back here too, thanks?"

They ate their dinner as Tess just sat there dumbfounded at every word that came out of Petey's mouth. She kept checking the time on her phone and wishing it would ring. It didn't matter who called, she just wanted an excuse to break away from him. But it never rang. Finally, dinner ended and Petey offered to walk her to her car.

"I had a great time tonight and the food was delicious. I bet you taste that good, too." Petey said clearly not getting the strong 'not on your life' vibe that Tess had been sending out all evening. Tess laughed at the ridiculous comment. "You're a clown. Next time I will make the reservations and don't forget to bring the breath mints."

"Why do you keep on dissing me wit the breath jokes? I brushed my teeth today. Anyway can I get a kiss, a hug, some kind affection?"

Was he for real, she thought? "Hell no, nigga. You wanna be a player, go be wit your bum ass girlfriend. You can get a tip though. Gargle before you come again wit your all day morning breath, skunk mouth." She said still not believing how corny he was.

"You want me to walk you to the car?" He asked really not wanting to let the night end.

"No no, I'm fine stinky mouth. You can do me a favor, though."

"What's that?" He asked excitedly.

"Take your dumbass home and brush that tooth."

Petey laughed. "You love me girl, hush up." He said as she got up from the table and left. He watched her walk away

They say I couldn't play football, I was too small.
They say I couldn't play basketball, I wasn't tall,
They say I couldn't bag chicks at all.
Now Every Day of My Life I Ball!

wishing that the night had gone better. Knowing that he had to tell the lieutenant about the date, his stomach turned a little.

They say I couldn't play football, I was too small.
They say I couldn't play basketball, I wasn't tall,
They say I couldn't bag chicks at all.
Now Every Day of My Life I Ball!

The Next King

Tess got into her car and took out her phone. She couldn't wait to tell Michaela all about the date. Hell, she still couldn't believe how bad it really had been. If it weren't for Mizz, she thought to herself, she would have walked out on that clown before they had even sat down. Michaela answered on the third ring.

"Hello, hey girl you know I can't wait to hear the scoop."

"Shit bitch, only scoop you going to hear is that I'm not fucking wit that clown ass nigga. I love Mizz but girl, I can't! I'm serious." Tess said, the pain of the night still fresh in her mind.

"Bitch! What happened?" Michaela wanted details.

"Girl, that nigga is fuking corny I swear. And the nigga tried to play me like I was some bird bitch or something, talking 'bout he got a girl like the nigga fly or something."

"What! Get the fuck outta here. Now I'm heated that bum ass nigga got some fuking nerve."

"Girl, I wanted to smack the shit out that dumb ass nigga. Then he stayed playing himself acting like I wanted him. I regret fuking wit the nigga. All cuz I luv your boy Mizz, anyway."

"That bitchss nigga is mad corny for that." Michaela said.

"Girl, for real he is a bitchass nigga I swear! But bitch, this is the ultimate. Oh my god, this nigga's breath smelled like chitlens, straight shit, hallway project piss."

Michaela laughed hard. "You crazy, that nigga's breathe smelled like that? Something must be wrong wit his

They say I couldn't play football, I was too small.
They say I couldn't play basketball, I wasn't tall,
They say I couldn't bag chicks at all.
Now Every Day of My Life I Ball!

stomach for real. I knew a dude name Eric that used to pick me and my girls up. He was my flunky. Girl, it would be below zero outside and you still had to let the window down. I swear, he had dead worms or some shit in his stomach, maggots and shit. Tess, the nigga would open up to yawn and flies would come out his mouth. Now you know he too old to have his mouth smelling like that."

Tess interrupted her before she got sick. "You know what bitch you need to stop."

"Ok then let me break the news to Mizz. I will call you lata bitch." Michaela said.

"Ok hoe, lata." Tess hung up the phone and drove home. She couldn't wait to be in her bed sound asleep and at last be able to forget about her night.

Dreading it but knowing she had to; she picked up the phone and called Mizz. As she waited for him to answer, she wondered how she was going to break the news about what Tess had said.

"Hello, what's good girl?" He got right to it. "What happen? Did he hit?"

Michaela took a deep breath before answering. "Bad news, babe, bad news."

"Aw shit, damn what the fuck!" He did not like the sound of that.

"I just have to give it to you straight. She said the nigga was mad corny and his breath smelled like shit and hallway piss."

She had painted a nasty mental picture. "Damnmmmn, that's crazy! Daaaaammmmmnn! Ewhhhh! But for real he does look like his face stinks. That's fucked up. I guess we on plan B then."

"Plan B?" She was confused. 'Was this some kind of

They say I couldn't play football, I was too small.
They say I couldn't play basketball, I wasn't tall,
They say I couldn't bag chicks at all.
Now Every Day of My Life I Ball!

military operation,' she thought to herself.

"Yea plan B. Long story." Not wanting to lose all the ground Tess had gained with Petey, he said, "Michaela, baby, she can't stop talking to Stank Breath until we resolve the problem, but it's all good. Tell Tess good looks but the show must go on; but in this case, it ain't over till the fire is put out."

"The fire is put out?" She said not understanding what Mizz was saying.

"Yea in his mouth," He laughed, trying to redirect his comment and keep Michaela from asking more questions.

"But it's all good. Tell Tess good looks. Tell her I luv her and thanks, the job will get done. I gotta run out and meet Razah. Baby, I will holla at you later."

"Gotcha babe. Everything ok?"

"Everything is the way it's supposed to be. I'm out babe I'll hit you later, sexy girl."

"Ok, baby." Michaela hung up not feeling right about how the call had gone. She needed to talk to Tess about it. She wasn't sure what to think of what Mizz had said and she didn't know what Tess would think, either. She called Tess to fill her in on the conversation.

"Hello, hey girl what's up?" Tess answered sounding wide awake.

"I'm feeling like I'm right in the middle of this wit you, Petey and Mizz. Check it out, when I told Mizz what was going on, he was like you couldn't stop talking to him 'cuz they have to resolve our problem'. Then he was like 'no matter, the job will get done'. What the fuck is going on?"

Tess sensed the worry in her friend's voice and didn't know what to say. "For real, I guess it's nothing. If I was

They say I couldn't play football, I was too small.
They say I couldn't play basketball, I wasn't tall,
They say I couldn't bag chicks at all.
Now Every Day of My Life I Ball!

you I wouldn't worry about it. You thinking too much and reading into something that don't need to be read into."

"Maybe you're right. But sorry to say Tess, he is a genius and he is never wrong and better to say he doesn't make mistakes. That's what scares me. A nigga like him always has an objective and a target for his mastermind ass. Its crazy cuz he gets what he wants, when and where he wants it, even who he wants; he conquers it all." They chatted for a few more minutes before hanging up and heading to bed. Neither of them slept very well thinking about Mizz, and Petey, or the so-called problem.

Deciding that his chances with Tess were pretty much over, Petey needed to find another way to get information on Mizz and his fam. He remembered meeting one of the crew at the Christmas party who had seemed like a potential target. In fact, he had even gotten a card from him. He went to his closet trying to remember what he had worn that night. Seeing the jeans from that night lying on the closet floor, he picked them up, pulled the card out of the back pocket and looked at the name on the card, Meneto. He remembered him now, a taller dude with a bald head and a goatee. Definitely not one of the leaders, he still seemed like a good option. A few seconds later, he dialed his number. He wasted no time and asked Meneto to meet him later to discuss a potential business opportunity. Meneto agreed.

They met up a few hours later at a local park. As Petey approached the park, he saw Meneto waiting for him on one of the basketball courts. "It's nice to see you again Meneto." Petey said, walking up. "Let me get right to the point. I know that you are in the inside and you not family but I feel like I can trust you. Not to be in your

They say I couldn't play football, I was too small.
They say I couldn't play basketball, I wasn't tall,
They say I couldn't bag chicks at all.
Now Every Day of My Life I Ball!

business but I see how these niggas is living and you should be living the same way. Something ain't right wit that picture. They clocking paper getting that money, but, my nigga I can cut you a sweeter deal than them tight ass niggas will ever give you, enough where you can expand and probably even start your own shit." Petey said trying get into Meneto's head.

Meneto's eyes widened. "Damn, where the fuck did you just come from? This is just what I was looking for. Trust them niggas getting that bread, feel me. They paying me straight but I know I ain't family so these muthafuckers could be paying me more. You know how much a week they make? Trust, Petey that nigga Mizz is a genius. That muthafuckas smarter than Bill Gates." Petey just stood there taking mental notes. "Nigga, last week he clocked 15 million in one week. He is a ghetto superstar for real and his shit is so tight, he will never get caught. I swear he is an irregular nigga. Fuck these house niggas but, if you wanna do business wit me I want 30% and you will only report to me and me only, you dig? Give me your other number." Meneto saw dollar signs in his head.

"Here you go." Petey could hardly believe how easy this had been.

"Oh yea." Meneto said, taking the card. "I will be in touch. Be safe." He turned and walked away. Petey watched him leave, then headed to his car and called the lieutenant.

"Hello?" the lieutenant answered.

"These wanna be slick muthafuckers is going down." Petey said proudly.

Later on that day at the pizza shop, Mizz met up with Razah to give him the lowdown on the Tess and Petey

They say I couldn't play football, I was too small.
They say I couldn't play basketball, I wasn't tall,
They say I couldn't bag chicks at all.
Now Every Day of My Life I Ball!

situation and discuss their next steps.

"Sonn, what's good b?" Razah said as Mizz entered the shop.

"Sonn, no happs sonn, no happs. Same shit, different toilet." Mizz said as they dapped each other.

"Wow, b what's really good? Anything poppin?"

"She said the nigga was awful my dude and the nigga's breathe smelled worse than elephant shit."

"Ewwwwwwwwwhhhhhh cuzin'. She is dumb funny sonn. But real talk, he look like every time I see him he got that white shit on the side of his mouth." Razah laughed.

"So I believe it sonn. Word."

"Plan B, sonn. Tell Leak's girl, Chantress, I need to holla at her b for real. I don't like or trust dude. This nigga is priority fam feel me. I swear on everything something is up wit this clown. I have that gut feeling, you dig. I want all access to this nigga phones, residence, the whip, bank accounts all that, all his B.I. my nigga. Razah I'm getting to the bottom of this my dude. Word." Mizz had already formed the plan in his mind.

"Sonn, I got you don't worry." Razah said knowing that he didn't have to say it. It was understood that they had each other's backs at anytime and through anything.

Meanwhile, Meneto was eager to get things started with Petey. He could smell the paper and was getting hungry for it. Meneto took out Petey's card and dialed his cell.

"Yo, what's good Meneto. How you?"

"Don't forget what we talked about. I'm definitely going to be next mothafuckas, feel me?"

"Just trust me. Just trust me and you will be good." Petey reassured him. 'Like taking candy from a baby,' he thought to himself as he snapped his phone closed.

They say I couldn't play football, I was too small.
They say I couldn't play basketball, I wasn't tall,
They say I couldn't bag chicks at all.
Now Every Day of My Life I Ball!

They say I couldn't play football, I was too small.
They say I couldn't play basketball, I wasn't tall,
They say I couldn't bag chicks at all.
Now Every Day of My Life I Ball!

Plan B

The next day on their way to school, Mizz and Razah discussed their current situation and their future.

"Sonn, what's good wit you this a.m. nigga?" Mizz asked as they walked.

"I'm chilling and shit b. Just tired as fuk, that all."

"Yo, I have been thinking bro. We made millions and millions of dollars and both of us don't ever gotta do anything again in our life time." Mizz said having been thinking about it all night.

"Yea, Mizz you right brotha. I was thinking the same shit the other day my nigga."

"I'm thinking about getting out the game and focusing on my career as a basketball player. You feel me? And leave this other stuff alone."

"Word brotha. I'm feeling your "g" right now b, word."

"Bro, for real what else do we have to prove especially while we on top? Let's not be like these other hustles before us, Rayful Edmonds, Frank Lucas, the list goes on and on. They wanted to wait till something popped off then they were fucked up. We don't need to do that bullshit, feel me? We straight now."

"I'm definitely feeling your gangsta. Sonn, what made you think of that cuz?" asked Razah.

"Cuz, what's the difference between a black man and a nigga?"

"What? Tell me sonn," Razah laughed as he tried to think of the answer.

"The nigga will continue to hustle when he is on top but then he gets caught. We not ignorant ghetto ass niggas,

They say I couldn't play football, I was too small.
They say I couldn't play basketball, I wasn't tall,
They say I couldn't bag chicks at all.
Now Every Day of My Life I Ball!

in that sense. We business men. Here is another example; you up by a touchdown wit a minute left in the game, why would you run or throw the ball to risk a fumble or interception, you would just take a knee right? Run the clock out and secure and win the game. Same shit wit us. Why risk it we on top?"

"Gotcha, gotcha, my nigg." Razah nodded

"Just something to think about sonn. I will holla at you after practice, in the meantime hit Chantress up see what's good wit her."

"No doubt b. Holla at you later sonn, word." As they walked in the front door of the school, they were greeted by their guidance counselor and both of their coaches.

"Hey guys just wanted to touch base wit you two because the school year is coming to an end; we want to see what your plans were for the summer," the guidance counselor said, eager for their answer.

"Both of you will be juniors next year and the scouts are hustling, asking questions about you both for a package deal," Razah's football coach said excitedly.

"Yes, I have never seen anything like this before and no one in this whole state has either. We all just wanna make sure that the both of you are seriously focused, that's all. Plus, we are very proud of you, in case you didn't already know," Mizz's basketball coach added.

Mizz spoke first. "We wanna succeed just as much as you want us to, please believe."

"We especially appreciate the support that you have for us; you guys are a really big part of our success." Razah added.

"Ok, thanks. Now get a move on to class before you guys are late." The guidance counselor said feeling

They say I couldn't play football, I was too small.
They say I couldn't play basketball, I wasn't tall,
They say I couldn't bag chicks at all.
Now Every Day of My Life I Ball!

reassured that the biggest things to ever happen to the
school had their heads in the right place.

Before parting ways and heading to class, they stopped,
leaning in to each other in a corner in the hallway. They
both felt their hearts beating a little too fast. "Nigga! For
sure, when I saw them all standing there I felt they was on
too us b, word." Mizz whispered.

"Sonn, I thought it was over for niggas, real talk."
Razah agreed.

Mizz took a deep breath. "Damnmnn, we going to get wit
Chantress tonight and see what is really good. I can't be
tripping like this and don't know what's up. Dooke, I will
holla lata." They heard the bell ring and they headed off to
class. After practice Mizz and Razah caught up with
Chantress and gave her the 411 on the Petey situation and
what they needed her to do. They felt like time was
running out and needed to get a handle on things sooner
than later.

"Hey baby girl?" Mizz said as he hugged Chantress.

"How you? Glad you could come out tonight. But here
is the scoop. You knew that Tess was chilling wit Petey."

"Ok, I see that clown around. Why she chilling wit
him?" She asked. "She too fly for him she need to be wit
me." She had always had a thing for her. "I don't trust that
nigga for some reason."

"So it ain't new news that she chilling wit that nigga.
You seen them, right?" Mizz continued.

"Nah, it ain't new news. I seen them several times."

"That's why we need your help." Razah said.
"Something ain't right wit that dude and we trying to
figure it out."

"Yo, ChanTess," Mizz said hoping that she got his

They say I couldn't play football, I was too small.
They say I couldn't play basketball, I wasn't tall,
They say I couldn't bag chicks at all.
Now Every Day of My Life I Ball!

point. "I think the nigga police. I don't know why, I just do. Something about his walk, he walk like he gotta take a shit. You know that police walk."

Chantress laughed. "You mad stupid. So what you want me to do? It's done."

"Well like I said before, Tess was chilling wit him. I told Michaela to ask Tess to chill wit him so we can see what he is about. Tess is extra fly. What dude won't tell Tess his business, feel me?" Mizz said, but Chantress interrupted him. "I knew there was a reason why she was chilling wit him. It's all coming clear now. I'm sorry, go head and finish what you was saying."

Mizz continued. "Well she said she can't fuck wit the nigga no more cuz he is unbearable and is extra corny. This when you come in; you have to just go wit the flow and flirt wit the nigga. Make him feel wanted and seduce him to get all the information you can. If it's none than it's none, but I know I'm right wit my instinct."

"I'm down," she said looking a little confused. "One problem, I'm not Tess?"

"Yes, you're Tess. We doing the mask shit. Michaela going to take the pics of her from every angle and Razah will upload the photos on the pc to make the mask. I picked up some special effects details from that director dude, Chase. I almost forgot, we need Michaela to get Tess to read that conference invitation so we can get the voice audio of Tess so you can practice sounding just like her."

"Ok Mizz, whenever you ready I will do it. Shit, I wanna know what's really good wit the fool now."

"No doubt sweetheart, it will be sooner than you think. Believe that, sooner than you think."

Not wanting to waste any time, Mizz met up with

They say I couldn't play football, I was too small.
They say I couldn't play basketball, I wasn't tall,
They say I couldn't bag chicks at all.
Now Every Day of My Life I Ball!

Chantress the very next day to put the plan into action. He hooked her up to the voice synthesizer, just like he had been shown by the director while out in Cali. He had her test out her voice and it sounded perfect, just like Tess. He and Razah listened on speaker phone as she called Petey to ask him out to chill.

Petey, always eager, answered the phone on the first ring.

"Hello, what's up girl?"

"Hey, how you doing sexy boy?" Chantress hoped she sounded just like Tess. "I was thinking about you just wondering if we can get up later to catch up. I really miss you."

"Shit girl, I know you miss me, I know you can't stop thinking about me either. I will do you a favor. Meet me at seven at the mall in the food court. Don't be late, my time is limited," Petey was letting her call to him get to his head.

"Ok, I will never be late for you boy. I can't wait to see you."

After she hung up, Mizz and Razah looked at each other, not believing what they just heard. "Holy shit! That nigga is dumb corny." Mizz laughed. "Is he serious? Wow, he really needs to knock it off; he playing himself."

"Ewhhhhh, word b, I see why shorty whop ain't wanna fuk wit that bum ass nigga." Agreed Razah.

"He is a lame ass nigga for real. Oh my god. Damn, he is LOC all the way."

"Wow. Nevertheless get Tress ready to be Tess." Mizz said as he took the mask out of the bag and handed it to Razah. Razah spent the next several hours making her up and molding the mask so that she looked just like Tess. After he was done, Mizz looked at her and shook his head in disbelief.

They say I couldn't play football, I was too small.
They say I couldn't play basketball, I wasn't tall,
They say I couldn't bag chicks at all.
Now Every Day of My Life I Ball!

"Tess make this dumb ass nigga feel wanted and boost his ego more cuz the sambo is really feeling himself, I hope he can walk thru the door." Mizz said as Chantress finished getting ready for her date.

"I got you baby. Trust me." She looked in the mirror and couldn't believe how good she looked. She practically wanted herself.

That night, Chantress found Petey waiting for her at the mall food court, just as they had discussed. Immediately she started gaming him. "Hey Petey, good to see you. Damn boy, you look causally fine tonight, how have you been?" She said trying to act just like she thought Tess would.

"Well you look different, in a good way of course. You, of course had to step your game up being next to me."

"I know. Right, cut it out now you doing too much dude." Sitting in their car outside, Razah and Mizz listened on thru the wire they had planted on Chantress. "Sonn, you believe this nigga dooke, do you actually hear his whack ass b?" Mizz shook his head.

"Razah sonn, word! It's a damn shame niggas like him exist." Razah agreed nodding his head.

"Word to mother sonn." Mizz stopped short as they heard Chantress's voice coming through the speakers again.

"I always wanted to tell you this. When I first saw you, did you see me staring at you?" She said touching his arm.

"I can't say I did."

"Well I was, I knew you were new in school and you didn't have any friends." Chantress looked up at him playfully making sure to use her long lashes and pert mouth to her advantage. " I wanted to be your friend," she purred.

They say I couldn't play football, I was too small.
They say I couldn't play basketball, I wasn't tall,
They say I couldn't bag chicks at all.
Now Every Day of My Life I Ball!

Petey smiled. "Shiitt, well let's make up for lost time. You can definitely be my friend!" he said laughing.

They say I couldn't play football, I was too small.
They say I couldn't play basketball, I wasn't tall,
They say I couldn't bag chicks at all.
Now Every Day of My Life I Ball!

Damn! Mmm, mmm, mmm!

The season was all most finished with just one more conference game left before the state tournament started. If Mizz and his team finished strong with one last win, for the first time in the school's history, they would be a number one seat in the tournament.

With just hours to go before the game, Mizz was going through his standard game day routine when the phone rang. He looked at the caller id and saw that it was Michaela. 'Wonder why she is calling,' he thought to himself before answering it. "Hello. Damn girl you calling mad early. You was thinking about me that much?"

"Hey baby, you know I was thinking about you. How can I not?" she said softly.

"All jokes aside. It's dumb early. You never call this early. You ok?" She swallowed hard. "I know you got a big game today, I really didn't wanna bother you wit it right now. But I have to. Baby I haven't gotten my period yet and I'm scared. I don't know what to do."

"Word! Say fucking Word! Michaela I was strapped and had the jimmy extra tight, feel me. Damn you like all the rest of these bitches. Got your fucking hand out cuz you see a nigga and see dollars signs, ain't that a bitch."

"Really Mizz, I wasn't saying anything. I was just letting you know I didn't get my period and I was scared," she said fighting back her tears. "But I see you insensitive to my feelings, you only care about Mizz. It's all good. I see a nigga real colors, you black rotten bastard, but you know what? You a sorry ass nigga. You going to lay down wit me, but you selfish muthafucker don't wanna take care of your responsibility. I'm good enough to fuck but not

They say I couldn't play football, I was too small.
They say I couldn't play basketball, I wasn't tall,
They say I couldn't bag chicks at all.
Now Every Day of My Life I Ball!

good enough to have a family wit. You a fucking dirtball ass nigga. Fuck you nigga!" She yelled into the phone before hanging up.

"Nah, hold on baby Michaela! Michaela!" He said but all he heard was dial tone. Michaela sat on her bed trying not to cry. Her pride refused her the satisfaction. She couldn't believe how Mizz had just spoken to her. She felt disrespected, used, abused and violated. 'How could Mizz be so insensitive,' she thought to herself as she buried her face into her pillow and started to cry. Three hours later, Razah looked at Mizz as they walked to school. He sensed by Mizz's body language that something was up.

"Sonn, what's good b, you got your head down moping and shit like your dog died or some shit. You forgot you got a big ass game tonight, the last conference game and it's for the number one seat in the tournament and you playing against that dude going to Georgia Tech? What's really good?"

"I know fam, I know b," Mizz responded not looking up.

"You don't seem into it at all today sonn. You straight?"

Mizz sighed. "I'm straight cuzo. I just got a lot on my mind sonn but I'm good b. What's poppin wit Chantress and sonn?

"She told me yesterday that they both coming to the game tonight."

"Word, word, ok, ok, you think he opening up to her yet sonn?"

"Shit, she bad as fuck. Wouldn't tell her you're too busy to get that ass," Razah laughed. " Real talk tell her something. Anyway b you gotta focus. You got a big game

They say I couldn't play football, I was too small.
They say I couldn't play basketball, I wasn't tall,
They say I couldn't bag chicks at all.
Now Every Day of My Life I Ball!

tonight."

"True, true, you right sonn. My man! You keeping my head leveled, no doubt bro. I got you." Mizz was starting to feel better and decided that he would deal with the Michaela situation after he took care of business on the court. But with just a few minutes before the tip off, Mizz couldn't stop thinking about Michaela. Razah, like every game time ritual, sat behind him on the bench so that they could chat, but this time Mizz still had the same grim look on his face from earlier today and wasn't talking. Razah noticed the crew in the stands and pointed them out to Mizz. "Sonn, there goes the crew as usual. Oh shit, look its Petey and Chantress."

"Sonn, I told she is going hard b, word. Damn, where is Michaela?" Mizz said looking all around the stands.
Razah hesitated before answering. "I haven't seen her sonn. I haven't seen her b." As the game began, Mizz continued looking around but there was still no sign of Michaela. Unable to completely focus on the game, Mizz, thinking of off court matters more than usual during his game, was yelling at his teammates, forcing shots and even turning the ball over. The coach, seeing that something was wrong with his star player, called a timeout.

"Timeout, please," the coach signaled to the ref. As the team approached the bench, he pulled Mizz towards him. "Mizz what's wrong? Have a seat on here and just relax. You're doing too much and you forcing plays. Just sit here for a minute and get your mind right." Mizz sat there with his head between his legs and his hands on his head. He could tell that what Michaela said to him earlier was majorly affecting him and his play. It's nothing the other team is doing, it's him. After about five minutes Mizz

They say I couldn't play football, I was too small.
They say I couldn't play basketball, I wasn't tall,
They say I couldn't bag chicks at all.
Now Every Day of My Life I Ball!

got his head together and got back into the game. He ended up with the game high, forty-two points, twelve assists and seven rebounds. Even more importantly, they won the game and for the first time in the school's history, secured a number one seat in the state tournament.

After the game Mizz called Michaela, but there was no answer. Meanwhile Petey and Chantress, still done up as Tess, stood in the parking lot chatting about their friendship.

"Hey Petey, we have been chilling for a while now, I'm really feeling you." Chantress started to move in for the kill. "I just hope you feeling the same way about me, cuz it won't be a good look if you not. I don't wanna get hurt."

"No, I understand. I don't wanna be deceitful. I have been thinking for awhile especially since you and I been chilling real hard. I wanna be completely honest wit you. I think I'm falling in love wit you. It's crazy for a g like me to do that but it can be done." Petey said, getting caught up in what he thought was a score with Tess.

Chantress looked at him and smiled, thinking to herself that this lame ass nigga should sit his corny ass down somewhere. But saying what she was thinking would not be a good idea. "Oh my god, really, I hoped you felt the same. I have a question for you since you know I'm giving you my heart. Tell me more about yourself. Like, do you have any secrets or something that you want to trust me wit." She had him hooked and knew that anything he had to hide he would tell her now. Buttering him up she said,

"Like, I was wondering, how do you have a nice car and fly clothes? You have no job."

"Ok," he said, throwing all pretense out the door, "I have to confess something to you, only cuz you are right I

They say I couldn't play football, I was too small.
They say I couldn't play basketball, I wasn't tall,
They say I couldn't bag chicks at all.
Now Every Day of My Life I Ball!

owe you at least some honesty from me. But, you have to always keep it real wit me cuz I see a big future wit us and I'm feeling you Tess. I'm an undercover cop, I'm telling you this cuz I don't want you to get caught up wit Mizz and his goons; they are going down."

She looked at him pretending to be surprised by his revelation. "What! Are you serious?" She laughed. "You're crazy! Mizz, his goons. What does that mean?"

He continued. "Those two innocent looking muthafuckas are the biggest drug dealers. I have a whole folder of their operation at my crib in the safe. I'll show you."

"Please do!"She said excitedly. "I gotta see this. I am so overwhelmed wit this information. So if you an undercover cop, who do you live wit?"

"Baby, I'm 22 years old. I have my own crib."

She couldn't believe he wasn't holding nothing back. "Damn, your secret is secure wit me trust!"

"So tell me about you?" he said looking into her eyes. Chantress thought she'd have a little more fun with him,

"Well, I'm a drug dealer and I help Mizz and Razah get money. I'm a runner." She answered honestly, knowing that he wouldn't believe her, especially as Tess.

He laughed. "You stupid. They ain't silly enough to have a sweet sexy girl like you selling no drugs for them. Nice try, I'm not that dumb."

"Aww, I know baby, I was just playing. So, on that note." She laughed. "I'm just a student. I'm not half as interesting as you. You a renegade. Damn that is so sexy, I'm really falling in love wit you." She said getting into his car. Twenty minutes later they arrived at his crib.

"You have a nice place, boo boo." Chantress said as she walked through the front door.

They say I couldn't play football, I was too small.
They say I couldn't play basketball, I wasn't tall,
They say I couldn't bag chicks at all.
Now Every Day of My Life I Ball!

"Thanks sweetheart, maybe so you can move in." He took her hand and led her into his bedroom. He climbed under the bed and pulled out the safe, typed his password in, and said his full name out loud, unlocking the voice activated lock. The safe opened and Petey pulled out the folder he had mentioned earlier.

"Damn baby, this shit is nice, and that safe is banging. I know you get money, real money." Chantress said.

"I do my best. Here is the folder I was telling you about. Look at all these niggas and check out this fine ass chick," he said pulling out a picture of Chantress as herself.

"All these muthafuckers going down."

"Damn, you really did your homework. You got everyone. I feel your gangster for real."

"So that's why I don't want you fucking wit these dumb asses cuz when we come, trust me we coming correct. All the evidence is there and I'm the only one that has this information. This is my case."

"Baby, thanks for the heads up. That's why I'm really feeling you. But, its late and I have a test in the morning. Can you bring me home, please?" She had accomplished her mission and knew she had to get this info back to Mizz, pronto."

"Sure, anything for you baby."

As they were leaving, Chantress went for one last bit of information. "I see you got two phones." she said. "You definitely balling. What's the other number? I don't have that one."

"That's my work phone. Of course you can have the number. I know you won't give it out."

They left his crib and headed back to the mall to drop off Tess to meet her mother.   Chantress opened the

They say I couldn't play football, I was too small.
They say I couldn't play basketball, I wasn't tall,
They say I couldn't bag chicks at all.
Now Every Day of My Life I Ball!

car door and looked back at Petey. "Hey Petey, I had an amazing night. very unforgettable," she said with a knowing smile. "I will call you tomorrow."

"The pleasure was all mine. But hold up mommy, do I get a kiss or some kind of affection?"

"I really want to. But, Petey, I am feeling you on a level I can't explain so I wanna make sure that this is right." Chantress said trying not too gag at the thought of kissing him. "So I wanna take things slow and do it the right way."

"I respect that. I will wait for your call tomorrow. Don't make me wait too long, though."

"Thanks again for tonight and please believe you will be on my mind and I will not make you wait too long. Goodnight, babe." She got out of his car and walked into the mall and immediately called Razah to tell him to get in touch with Mizz as soon as possible. Razah called her back a few minutes later and told her to meet them at the spot. Chantress arrived at the spot a short while later. She saw Mizz and Razah standing there each with a crazy look on their faces like they had both seen a ghost. "Yo, my nigga you won't believe this shit." She was breathing hard. "Damn I'm fucked up right now."

"What up?" Mizz said in a worried tone.

"Niggas, that sneaky black mothafucka is undercover."

Mizz shook his head. "Muthafucker."

"Razah sonn, ain't that a bitch? What do we do know?" Razah asked shaking his head.

"I knew that nigga was something. Damnmmmnnn! That's fucked up and the nigga was trying to infiltrate. Wow!" Mizz's mind was reeling.

They say I couldn't play football, I was too small.
They say I couldn't play basketball, I wasn't tall,
They say I couldn't bag chicks at all.
Now Every Day of My Life I Ball!

"The nigga knows everything, but he thinks we selling drugs, not the legit stuff we're dealing. He got folders on all of us, it's crazy." Chantress said.

"Tell me everything you know. I will take that and see how to maneuver, flip it and bounce it." Mizz said with mind already working on a plan. "That nigga thinks he smarter than us. He violated and try to come into our circle. Chantress, just keep chilling wit him. Then soon he will feel my mothafuckin G!" Mizz's voice echoed. "Good work baby, it's late. I will holla at you lata."

"No doubt. We good. I know you will handle this nut ass nigga."

"Trust he will begin to itch very soon. Trust me, it's nothing. You know me."

"Word. Goodnight baby." They hugged her and she left. After she left, they chatted about what had just happened. "Wow, sonn that is crazy. How can niggas live wit themselves doing fuk boy shit like that? That is unbelievable to me." Razah said as they watched Chantress drive off.

"Bro, don't be surprised. That's just how some people live, no loyalty to nothing. I bet that nigga Republican."

"I know how you get down sonn. So you know I'm down for whatever you need."

"I'm not going to school tomorrow. I'm going to get one of Leaks girl's cars and follow him b. It's on now my nigga for real. Sonn, I'm dumb tired I will holla at you in the a.m."

"100 my nigg." They dapped each other up and headed home.

Mizz and Razah lay on their beds looking at the ceiling, wondering what the fuck had just happened. They

They say I couldn't play football, I was too small.
They say I couldn't play basketball, I wasn't tall,
They say I couldn't bag chicks at all.
Now Every Day of My Life I Ball!

were both disgusted at the recent turn of events. Both unable to sleep, they thought about their next move.

They say I couldn't play football, I was too small.
They say I couldn't play basketball, I wasn't tall,
They say I couldn't bag chicks at all.
Now Every Day of My Life I Ball!

Caught Slippin'

Bright and early the next morning, Mizz set himself up in an abandoned building across the street from Petey's crib. He watched him through a telescope that he had pointed through a broken window. Focusing in on Petey's bedroom, he caught him opening the safe and pulling the paper work out. He looked it over for a moment and put it back. Mizz was still in disbelief at what was happening, but he had seen what he needed to see and bounced.

The rest of the day was a blur. His mind was a real mess and felt like it was going a hundred miles an hour. With the team being the number one seed in the tournament, the championship game, and the beef with Michaela, this bullshit with Petey was practically driving him insane. But he knew had to stay focused. The next morning, he contemplated whether or not he should call Michaela. He knew it would probably not be a good, but he called her anyway.

"Hello." Her voice always sounded so sweet.

"Hello Michaela, what's up? How are you?" he said in an almost apologetic voice.

"Good morning Mizz, I have to let you know before you go any further. I'm not in the talking mood, I'm preparing for my speech at the conference."

"Damn, the speech ain't till next week and plus it's dumb early in the a.m. Why you doing that? Anyway, look babe, I'm really sorry I was being a dick head. I had a lot on my mind so I wasn't being considerate of your feelings, believe me."

"Mizz, thanks but for real for real" She interrupted wanting the conversation to end. "I'm not feeling you. You

They say I couldn't play football, I was too small.
They say I couldn't play basketball, I wasn't tall,
They say I couldn't bag chicks at all.
Now Every Day of My Life I Ball!

should set me aside. I will never forget you but I need my space. You play on a basketball team and there is no " I" in team right? Take your own advice. It ain't always about Mizz. Hey, you took up enough of my time. Good luck on Saturday. Please don't call me. I'll call you. Have a wonderful day." Michaela hung up the phone feeling no remorse, leaving Mizz in definite 'wow' form and thinking to himself that this really wasn't his week.

Later on that morning as Mizz and Razah walked to school, they spotted Meneto and Petey walking into one of the project buildings. They looked at each other in disbelief at what they had just seen. "Sonn, did you see that shit kid?" Razah asked knowing that Mizz had.

"Yea, what the fuck is good wit that b? For now don't worry about it. After school go to the spot and tap the nigga phone and we will see what's good." Mizz sounded more together than he felt.

"Bro, I see why you never trusted that muthafucker Meneto anyway. Something is up for real. Something's gotta give."

"Dude, they doing something." Mizz agreed. "They cutting some type of deal cuz Meneto knows there's no bugs or anything inside there, but what they don't know is that at the table there is a camera in the clock sonn. Sonn bust it, call a meeting and I will be there after practice. Holla back, and hey," Mizz snapped his fingers, "just family."

After practice Mizz headed straight to the spot. Leak and the rest of the fam was already there waiting for him. Mizz and Razah filled them on the weekend's events and having spotted Petey and Meneto together when walking to school that morning.

They say I couldn't play football, I was too small.
They say I couldn't play basketball, I wasn't tall,
They say I couldn't bag chicks at all.
Now Every Day of My Life I Ball!

"Fam, what's good everybody? I won't keep you niggas much longer. I know time is money and we all gotta hit, so here is the scenario: this weekend is a big weekend, especially for me. It's like NBA all star weekend in case you d idn't know the festivities, the championship game, everything that goes wit it." His lowered his voice. "But, you muthafuckers didn't know this, your boy Meneto is infiltrated."

Leak looked at him. "He what?"

"Yea, that sneaky muthafucker is in the process of cutting a side deal wit that nigga Petey and he think he going to get away wit it."

"Damn, I feel like shit. I brought the nigga in and he treating me like a 2 dollar hoe. I'm going to smack that nigga wit a raw steak sonn, He can't even use ice cubes. He going to need a big ass piece of ham hock to put on this face, word." Leak said pounding his fist into his hand.

"Ewwwwwwwwwwwwwwwh cuzin, damn that shit sound like it going to hurt." Razah said cringing.

"Why nigga? Why would you do some ghetto shit like that anyway, sonn? Damn you ghetto Leak, all you going to do is bring more heat to us." Mizz cautioned.

"Come on Leak, we business men. We off the nigga gangster shit b. We about getting the money. So everyone is on the low, low for a while, so no dealing, no nothing. Say we been dry cuz I'm focused on the tournament and we ran out. We gotta wait. Tell him the other connect you got is that white girl, feel me. If he bites, that's how we gonna get that bitch ass nigga."

"No doubt, I will tell him that cuz he know how I use to hustle and get it in." Leak said.

"Yea no doubt, wit Meneto knowing that I don't fuck

They say I couldn't play football, I was too small.
They say I couldn't play basketball, I wasn't tall,
They say I couldn't bag chicks at all.
Now Every Day of My Life I Ball!

wit that white girl, he will feel that you and him are down and taking a side deal wit him. Give him two keys. No, front him those keys so there is no trace back to you. Outta respect, he will tell you who he selling the shit to. He is your man. I saw on the camera and heard Petey and Meneto talking about being the next king and shit. Wait a couple days then he will come to you on the re-up and hit him wit that shit kid."

"This nigga is crazy. I can't believe this fuck nigga. He going to pay." Leak said feeling Mizz's plan.

"What you can't believe that nigga ain't family and you can't gratify insanity. He is a fuck nigga. You can't control what someone else thinks or acts; you can only control you and your actions. What do you expect from a suburb Uncle Tom Republican tea party ass nigga? That type of nigga will tell his own mother to shut up, so why will you think that grimy nigga will respect you? He don't even respect his self. Fuck it, everything is everything, just no sells. I gotta prepare my speech for the convention on Sunday, see you niggas later." Mizz had other things on his mind. He headed home to work on his speech.

Petey dialed Chantress's number for the fifteenth time in two days. She had been ignoring his calls, but not wanting him to get suspicious, she finally picked up.

"Hello?"

"Wow, you finally answered my call. No calls from you or nothing huh? Babe you forgot about me? Dammmnn." Petey said practically whining.

"Babe, how can I forget you? What do you think, I just say things cuz it sounds good. I have been mad busy wit a lot of homework. How's your investigation going, baby?"

They say I couldn't play football, I was too small.
They say I couldn't play basketball, I wasn't tall,
They say I couldn't bag chicks at all.
Now Every Day of My Life I Ball!

"The investigation is crazy. I haven't seen anyone in the street or even heard anything."

"I thought it came to an end cuz I haven't seen them or heard from them either. Especially Michaela hasn't spoken about them. Plus you said you wanted me to stay away from them anyway, so I was listening to you."

"That's what I'm talking about, a woman that's submissive." She could almost hear him smiling and nodding his head. "That's right though" he laughed. "Hold on babe I gotta handle something. I will give you a call back."

"Ok, call me back. I miss you." She hung up the phone still not believing how corny he really was. She couldn't wait for his sorry ass to be out of the picture, however that might be. Petey hung up and called Meneto on the phone that Mizz and Razah had tapped earlier.

"Yo." Petey said as Meneto answered.

"What's up amigo?"

"What's going on, where the fuk you niggas been hiding and shit? I have been driving by the block, the spot, no one is around. What is really good?"

"I know, I was wondering the same thing, I will touch Leak in a second. You know I gotta text him. I wanna meet up wit the dude."

"Ok, holla at me after you get up wit him, asap." Petey said getting nervous that something might be up.

"I got you." Meneto hung up and immediately texted Leak, telling him to meet him up the boulevard in thirty minutes. Leak replied that it was cool and he would meet him there. Leak looked at his cell and read the text again. He smiled to himself. This was the text he had been waiting for. Twenty minutes later, he sat in his car waiting

They say I couldn't play football, I was too small.
They say I couldn't play basketball, I wasn't tall,
They say I couldn't bag chicks at all.
Now Every Day of My Life I Ball!

for Meneto to arrive. Meneto arrived right on time. "Yo! Where you niggas been at? I'm hit, I need paper bad! The mortgage, cars, kids school, all that. What's up my friend."

"Bro, bro, I know I know. The last batch is done, and the only one that knows how to make it is you know who! And the nigga is mad busy right now and that ain't his focus."

"Damn man, I knew this would happen! Fuk, what am I going to do? I will do anything I'm so hit. I'm dying over here my dude."

"But , my nigga don't worry. You know I'm a hustler I always got something poppin. It's about if you want in."

"Nah, Leak I told you I was hit. I will do anything. We straight."
Leak glared at him. "We? What you mean we? You got a buyer? You don't even know what's poppin. You doing side deals?"

"I have to. We have nothing."
Leak knew who that 'buyer' was but he had to ask, "Ok, well anyway who's your buyer? Can you trust him?"

"Petey is my buyer."

"Word, that young nigga got bread like that? Well bust it I got that white girl two keys, 28 a key. Can you dig it? Better yet I will front you the keys cuz we in a drought. You just give me the money when we back on."

Meneto couldn't believe his ears. "You serious, I swear you my man. We should be straight."
They dapped each other up and broke out. As he walked away, Meneto called Petey and told him what's good and that they needed to meet. They agreed to meet on the track at Holy Cross. Fifteen minutes later, Meneto stood anxiously waiting for Petey to arrive. He still couldn't

They say I couldn't play football, I was too small.
They say I couldn't play basketball, I wasn't tall,
They say I couldn't bag chicks at all.
Now Every Day of My Life I Ball!

believe how cool Leak had been. He was sure Petey would feel the same.

"What's up Petey? How you brotha?" Meneto said as Petey approached.

"Well it depends what you tell me first then I can tell you how I'm feeling."

"Well that's on you and how you take it. Bottom line, it's getting money." Meneto said rubbing his fingers together.

"You are so right. So what's the deal?"

"Ok, this is the deal dude, its drought you know, that's why you haven't seen niggas around and shit. In case you didn't know that sonn. Dude mad busy and can't do anything and he is the only one that knows how to make the shit. You know who I'm talking 'bout. But here is the other option, Leak got two keys of that white girl, twenty-eight a full bird."

"Damn, that's high for each one." Petey said, not believing his luck. "Whatever ok. I'm done. White girl come give me head. No matter, let's get this money, just tell me where to meet."

Meneto ain't shit, he was planning to keep the money and he was just fucking Petey wit the price. He was a real dirtball muthafucker. "Let's do it the night of the state championship game, no one will be around and we can swap out. I will be the next king of this shit. We will be getting that money and start our own shit, you understand?"

"You right, we will start wit this. Where do you have in mind to swap?" Petey asked.

"Let me think for a sec about it, shit has to be somewhere secure and not a lot of traffic around. I got it. They were building a lab off Burton Street. I was going to

They say I couldn't play football, I was too small.
They say I couldn't play basketball, I wasn't tall,
They say I couldn't bag chicks at all.
Now Every Day of My Life I Ball!

set up the computer system so I got the key."

"Cool, that's what it is then. We will holla later.

"My nigga." They dapped each other up and headed their separate ways.

Meneto called Leak and told him it's a done deal.

"What's good? Why you calling me? You know to text me," Leak answered sounding annoyed.

"I'm just letting you know it's a go my nigga. I told him to meet me at the place where I'm doing the new security system at on Burton the night of the game."

"Ok, call me at 6:45 and I'll give you directions where it will be cuz. I can't meet you. I will be at the game."

"Again good looking I got you. I really owe you." Meneto said.

"Nah, you gotta take care of your bills. Handle that brotha and when you on your feet I know you got me. You straight. holla at me, Sonn. I'm out."

"My nigga." Meneto said as he hung up.

Leak called up Mizz after hanging up with Meneto and told him to meet him as soon as he could. Leak was happy to be working under Mizz. Anyone else wouldn't have seen Petey coming and they would have all been facing serious time. Looking at this watch, he realized he only had a short time before it was time to meet up with Mizz. As he arrived at the spot, Mizz was already there eager to hear what Leak had to say. He could tell from Leak's smile that it was all good.

"Damn nigga, what you all smiling about cuzo?"

"It's about to be a rap. That nigga fucking wit it sonn. He is fucking wit it hard sonn." Leak said sounding like his usual gangster self.

"You told him to go to the replica drug lab, right?"

They say I couldn't play football, I was too small.
They say I couldn't play basketball, I wasn't tall,
They say I couldn't bag chicks at all.
Now Every Day of My Life I Ball!

"Yo Mizz, for real that nigga told me cuz, he had keys to the spot already and it was secure cuz 'member the nigga was putting in the security system."

"Ewhhhh cuzin, he really 'bout to be fucked. There's scales and all types of drug paraphernalia in that muthafucker, sonn. Word. Shit when them niggas get there they will be in for the time of their fuck up ass lives, snake bastards good for them fuk niggas." Mizz said shaking his head and smiling.

"Everything is everything b, you can just chill now and get ready for your game cuz and be focused. Niggas got it over here. Family trust b, worddddd. We will never let anything happen to you sonn, family first." Leak said hoping to assure Mizz that he nothing more to worry about.

"Good look Leak! Good look. I luv you nigga, word life."

"You and the family are my heart." Leak said tapping his heart with his right fist. "Peace out cuz." They bumped fists and left.

Feeling a little revived from his conversation with Leak, Mizz called Razah to tell him what was what. Things seemed to be looking a little better, but he had still had a lot on his plate.

He told Razah about the meeting with Leak and about the dumb ass Meneto.

"Yea!" Razah was relieved to hear that things might work themselves out.

"We good." Mizz said.

"No doubt." Razah agreed.

"Everything will be in place."

"Cool."

"Holla back." Mizz hung up the phone and continued

They say I couldn't play football, I was too small.
They say I couldn't play basketball, I wasn't tall,
They say I couldn't bag chicks at all.
Now Every Day of My Life I Ball!

walking home. He breathed a little easier as he refocused his mind on the upcoming championship game. The championship game arrived and everything they worked for all season came down to this one game. The place was packed with fans, college scouts, NBA scouts, and anyone that was somebody. Razah looked up at the score clock as the team came out of the locker room. He got up and walked toward the back, tapped Leak and told him to make the call. Leak got up and walked out to the lobby.

"Hello." Meneto answered.

"Yo, you inside?" Leak whispered into the phone.

"Yea."

"Iaght, go to the back and look in the cabinet behind the sink. There's a brief case wit the joint and something special for you always looking out for me when times get ruff."

Meneto followed his instructions and found the case.

"Word!! Ok, hold up let me open it up. Damn, blonde and heroic man too, sonn."

Leak looked at his phone. "You talking crazy sonn, I'm getting off the phone. I don't know what the fuck you talking 'bout. Peace. Hit me when you get them collard greens from your people crib."

"You right, I will holla."

In the briefcase, there were two kilos of cocaine and one kilo of heroin, a little gift from Leak to make sure both them niggas ended up underneath the jail for the bullshit they did. Razah, peaked out the locker room and Leak gave him the sign that everything was set. Meneto looked at the three keys sitting in front of him. Leak had definitely come through and hooked him up. Now that he had the stash, he called Petey to come meet him.

They say I couldn't play football, I was too small.
They say I couldn't play basketball, I wasn't tall,
They say I couldn't bag chicks at all.
Now Every Day of My Life I Ball!

"Hello," Petey answered from his car outside the lab.

"You here?" Meneto asked. "Come inside."

Everything seemed to be working out. Now, all that was left was for Mizz to do what he did best. Razah looked at the clock and called Mizz to let him know that it was his turn.

"Son, the game is starting in twenty minutes. Your team just came out to warm up. So hurry up."

"I will sonn," Mizz said. "I will be there before game time and make a grand entrance, feel me sonn!! Like Willis Reed, dude. Iaght aahahahahaha." Mizz hung up and breathed. He then dialed 911.

"Hello, can I please speak to Lieutenant Stevens? It's an emergency. Hello Lieutenant, how your day going today?" Mizz asked casually.

"I'm fine. Who is this?" the lieutenant asked. "And what do you want? They told me it was an emergency. This sounds like some bullshit. Again, who is this?" the lieutenant was not in the mood to deal with any prank calls. Mizz changed his tone. "That is not important right now!" he yelled into the phone. "What's important is that you listen very carefully to what is going on."

"What!" the lieutenant yelled back. "Who the fuck is this? You don't know who you fucking wit."

"Anyway, if you were fucking listening you ignorant muthafucker. Now you got shit popping off. Stop the tuff guy shit and pay attention."

Lieutenant pointed to one of the other officers and told him to trace the call. After a few seconds the officer called out that the call was coming from Petey's house. They sat there in suspense listening to what would come next.

The lieutenant took a deep breath. "Ok, I got you what's

They say I couldn't play football, I was too small.
They say I couldn't play basketball, I wasn't tall,
They say I couldn't bag chicks at all.
Now Every Day of My Life I Ball!

up. How can I be of assistance?"

"That's what I'm talking about, you must of traced the call and see I'm calling from one of your employee's house. Look, go to the monitor in your office and turn to channel 8. You will see one of your undercovers doing a big drug transaction worth about just a little, no, a lot of money. But he is dirty. I'm not trying to tell you how to do your job but you should go down there. 800 Locust and handle that. Good day officer." Mizz hung up the phone and hustled over to his next stop.

"What the fuck was that?" The lieutenant looked at his officers, who were just as stunned as he was. "Check that fucking monitor and I am going down there. Hit me on the cell to tell if you see any transaction before I get there. One of you two go and check out Petey's house, too. This is some wild bullshit. What the fuck, but, whatever you do don't call Petey. If this is true, I will deal wit that sneaky black muthafucker myself! Fuck!" He yelled still not believing that he might have to arrest one of his own men before the day was through.

As the lieutenant was headed over to the address that Mizz had given him, his officer called him telling him that he saw Petey and some other guy on the monitor and that there was definitely something going down. Pulling up to the building, the lieutenant was shocked when he spotted Petey's car parked outside. Although completely fucked up by all this, he didn't forget his job. He told the other officers not to move until there had been an actual transfer of the money and drugs. They waited until they got word from those watching the monitor back at the station. The lieutenant sat in his car and waited, thinking to himself 'black bitch ain't this some shit.'

They say I couldn't play football, I was too small.
They say I couldn't play basketball, I wasn't tall,
They say I couldn't bag chicks at all.
Now Every Day of My Life I Ball!

Meanwhile, Meneto and Petey were in the lab about to make the transaction. They dapped each other up and with no idea what was about to happen made the exchange.

"What up bro, you got the paper?" Meneto asked.

"Of course I do bro, you got the product?" Petey answered picking up a briefcase he had brought in with him.

"All here, baby." Meneto said lifting his own briefcase and setting it on the table.

The lieutenant got the signal and was just about to bust the door down when one of his officers radioed him to hold up because Petey's phone was ringing.

Meneto looked at Petey. "Bro, your phone is ringing."

"What? My phone ain't ringing." He tried to play it off.

Meneto sensing something was up told him. "Answer your fucking phone."

"Ok, ok, Peter Sampson."

"Who the fuck is Peter Sampson? What the fuck this seem like some funny shit." Meneto reached into his coat and grabbed his gun feeling like this might have been a setup. Petey answered his phone. Mizz started the tape recorder to record Petey as he answered the phone. "This is Mizzier Sanders." Petey wasn't at all surprised. "Good luck at your game. I will be there in a little while to support you. I was wondering when you were going to make this call. How did you get this number?"

"You didn't actually think that I would let you get away wit this, did you?"

"If you wanna set up a meeting we can definitely do that. I got what you need." Petey said hoping Mizz would take the bait.

They say I couldn't play football, I was too small.
They say I couldn't play basketball, I wasn't tall,
They say I couldn't bag chicks at all.
Now Every Day of My Life I Ball!

"Oh really, so where are you now?" Mizz asked even though he knew exactly where he was.

"I'm at home lying on my bed resting then going to the game." Petey said trying to sound relaxed.

"Knock it off nigga, I doubt that." Mizz snapped back.

"You not a good business man I see that already, if you were at home we would be having this discussion face to face you silly mothafuckas." With that, Mizz hung up wondering what Petey was thinking as he did. Petey stood there in disbelief. Meneto looked at him wondering what the fuck was going on and debating whether or not to shoot. Just outside the door, the lieutenant was sick of waiting. 'Fuck it,' he said to himself as he prepared to break down the door.

Mizz typed in the pass code to the safe and played the tape of Petey's voice saying his full name to access the safe. He grabbed all the files that Chantress talked about and left. He had been careful not to disturb anything else so when he closed the front door behind him, the house looked as if no one had been there.

A few blocks away, the lieutenant covered his ears as the front door to the lab exploded open. Standing in the middle of the room of what appeared to be a drug factory, Petey and Meneto looked dumbfounded. Seconds later they were surrounded by police officers who were telling them to freeze and asking if there was anyone else. Petey looked at his fellow officers and muttered

"Muthafuckers."

"Suck ass muthafucker." Meneto said to himself as looked around the lab and saw nothing but blue.

"Freeze you, especially you!!! You black muthafucker." The lieutenant pointed at Petey. "What you

They say I couldn't play football, I was too small.
They say I couldn't play basketball, I wasn't tall,
They say I couldn't bag chicks at all.
Now Every Day of My Life I Ball!

got to say for yourself you useless piece of shit?"

"I got him, Lieutenant." He replied. "We straight bro. I got this good for nothing scumbag!"

Meneto just glared at him. "Petey, you sneaky bitch ass nigga, I knew I shouldn't have trust your sneaky ass muthafucker." The lieutenant's phone rang. He answered it and listened closely, all the while never taking his eyes off of Petey. "Lieutenant we are here at Petey's house there is no sign of anything or anyone and definitely no signs of false entry. You sure someone was here?" The officer on the other end of the phone asked.

"Damn! You sure?" Lieutenant shook his head. "This is fucked up. Thanks though, good work."

Disgusted with the situation, lieutenant turned his attention back to Petey. "Shiiiiiiiittttttt, now what were you saying you sorry muthafucker? You played yourself, the unit, and especially me. The whole time you was selling drugs or buying drugs trying to use them poor mothafuckin kids. You should be fucking shot. Look around here. There are scales and shit in here, fucking drug lab. What the fuck is in the briefcases?" He picked them up and dumped their contents out onto the table. "Damn, heroin, cocaine and money. What the fuck, you niggas going under the jail for this shit, muthafuckers." Petey put up his hands. "I promise everything I said is true." He thought for a moment. "Ok then check my house, under my bed there's a safe with all the information you need in it." The lieutenant decided to give Petey one last chance. "Ok, hold up. 10-4, 10-4," he said into his radio.

"Yes sir." The officer on the other end answered.

"You guys still over at Petey's crib?"

"Yea, we still here what's up?"

They say I couldn't play football, I was too small.
They say I couldn't play basketball, I wasn't tall,
They say I couldn't bag chicks at all.
Now Every Day of My Life I Ball!

"I want you to check something out. Go to the bedroom, underneath the bed there's a safe."

"You got it boss." A minute passed while the officer followed his directions. "Hold on, ok I see it. It's open. Wow, you will never believe this lieutenant, you won't believe this!"

"What is it? I can believe anything now! Give it to me raw!" he demanded.

"There are three keys of heroin, two keys of cocaine, and three pounds of weed plus two scales. Wait a sec, there's more here. We've got three silencers and two 9's and the serial numbers are shaved off." The officer whistled. "What the fuck was Petey doing?"

The lieutenant was stunned. Looking at Petey he said, "You gotta be outta your fucking mind. I'm at a loss for words." To the officer on the line he said, "Good work! Good work!" He then walked over to Petey and got right up into his face. "Wow this is crazy, mad drugs at your house. You tried to play me again." he said, his face only an inch from Petey's.

"What the hell you talking about drugs at my crib? What the fuck you mean?" Petey couldn't believe that this was happening. "That shit ain't mine I swear!" he yelled.

"You going to do me like that."

Ignoring Petey's words, the lieutenant motioned to the other officers. "Read these niggas their rights. You both are under arrest." He stepped back and put out his hand. "And Petey give me your fucking badge you piece of shit. You're going right where you belong." The officers walked over to Petey and Meneto and cuffed them.

They say I couldn't play football, I was too small.
They say I couldn't play basketball, I wasn't tall,
They say I couldn't bag chicks at all.
Now Every Day of My Life I Ball!

New Life

With minutes before game time, Mizz finally arrived
and headed to the locker room to suit up. Everyone was
wondering where he was when he hadn't shown for warm
ups. The commentators played it up doing their best to add
drama to the moment, and just like he had told Razah he
would, Mizz made his grand entrance onto the court with
just two minutes left before tipoff. The crowd went nuts.
TV reporters compared it to when Willis Reed of the New
York Knicks made his grand entrance during the NBA
finals. The stage had been set for what would prove to
Mizz's best game to date. From the opening tipoff, he was
unstoppable and without a doubt, the best player on the
floor and in the country.

When the fourth quarter ended, he had racked up fifty-
five points, seventeen assists and fourteen rebounds, a
career high and the best triple double of his young career.
Fans poured onto the floor chanting, "Mizz! Mizz!" He
had won the state championship, just like everyone had
thought he would. Shortly after the game, to top off his
unbelievable season, he was awarded the MVP of the
tournament. He raised the trophy into the air and looked
into the stands, stopping short when he saw her shining
there, smiling like a diamond, with the cameras flashing all
around her. It was Michaela.

After all the interviews and autograph signing, Razah
waited for Mizz to congratulate him and talk about what
happened earlier. "My nigga," he said hugging Mizz. "You
did it sonn, you brought the chip here first time in school's
history. We both on top on the world right now. We going
to be on Sports Illustrated for real. We came a long way

They say I couldn't play football, I was too small.
They say I couldn't play basketball, I wasn't tall,
They say I couldn't bag chicks at all.
Now Every Day of My Life I Ball!

from nothing to something, believe that bro."

"Word up b. We been through it all, fam and we stuck together thru it all. And we still stay humble and ready for anything bro, word. But, check it b I saw Michaela." Mizz said smiling.

"Word b, iaghtaaaaaaaaaaaah. But my nigg it's a done deal sonn. Them niggas is hit real talk. It's over for them both. Great plan my nigga, great plan. You a genius I swear."

"I told you fuk them suck as niggas, they got what they deserved, for real sonn. I feel so relieved though. Punk ass, bitch ass niggas."

"Yo, while you were interviewing, I saw the shit on the breaking news about them assholes. The kids are going crazy here cuz they saw Petey. You know that nigga was 26 years old. Dumb old, that nigga was really trying to get niggas."

"I know right, where you saw that shit at?"
Razah interrupted Mizz before he could finish. "I saw the shit in the lobby where the concession stand shit at."

"That's crazy. Oh well it's a doooooozzeee for them niggas, fuk it lets move on, its water underneath the fucking bridge. Fuk them, they tried to fucks us so we fucked them, jealous muthafuckers."

"It's a rap especially for what they got caught wit, buying, selling, intent to distribute, school zone, and the shit at Petey house, it's a Reynolds for them niggas. Wrap it up," Razah said laughing. "You know what I mean. Fuk them niggas."

"Damn sonn. Leak literally took them to ecstasy cuzin', word.'

Razah laughed. "You dumb stupid cuz. Them

They say I couldn't play football, I was too small.
They say I couldn't play basketball, I wasn't tall,
They say I couldn't bag chicks at all.
Now Every Day of My Life I Ball!

bitchass niggas under the fucking jail dooke."

"True, anyways."

They continued to chat as they walked back to Mizz's crib. Things had come full circle for them. They had nothing more to worry about and now they could focus on what to do about their future. Money would never been an issue again and it looked as if their dreams of playing pro ball might come true. Just as they arrived back at his crib, Mizz's phone rang. He looked at the number and couldn't believe it. It was Michaela. They hadn't spoken since their last encounter on the phone, which had ended badly.

"Hello, yeah." Mizz answered.

"Hello Mizz, it was good seeing you tonight. You looked good." She sighed. "I'm going to keep this short and sweet cuz I know you just won and I want you to enjoy your celebration wit your teammates and friends. But, Mizz we need to talk about us, it really important."

"Thanks sexy, it was good seeing you tonight as well and I was surprised and happy at the same time. It made me feel complete and I do I agree we need to talk asap."

"I'm going away wit my parents for a week on a family emergency, so I won't be able to talk. But, I tell you what, we have the conference next week and we can talk and catch up wit everything then."

"That's a great idea, I hope everything is well wit your family. I will say a prayer for you all. I look forward to the convo cuz we need it. I got some things I need to get off my chest anyway. You my girl. Michaela talk to you soon babe."

"No doubt, thanks, I miss you Mizz. Talk to you soon. Love you."

Mizz hung up the phone looking dumb happy grinning

They say I couldn't play football, I was too small.
They say I couldn't play basketball, I wasn't tall,
They say I couldn't bag chicks at all.
Now Every Day of My Life I Ball!

from ear to ear. He and Razah then headed over to the to celebrate with the fam. As they arrived, the lights and shit are turned off in the club while everyone waited to surprise Mizz when he walked in through the front door.

He entered the club with Razah following behind. Before he could ask why the lights were out, all his fam jumped out yelling surprise. He turned and looked at Razah who just shrugged and smiled. Mizz looked around and saw not only his fam, but some fine looking ladies talking to his crew. Leaked walked up and put his hand on his back. "Surprise brotha, this all for you, strippers from Jamaica, Brazil, Puerto Rico, whatever you like and want. It's all here. You deserve it. Fuk these bitches. Hard work plays off." Leak laughed.

Everyone gathered around and congratulated Mizz. They started chanting "speech!" Not wanting to disappoint, he stood up and gave a little speech of his appreciation.

"I'm glad and so lucky to be sharing this opportunity wit people that care about me and love me. My fam, you niggas been here for me when we didn't have shit." He turned and looked at the strippers. "I appreciate these sexy chicks, but I'm good." He said smiling. "You horny niggas enjoy. I'm just happy we here together safe and sound, feel me."

"You always got some good and clever shit to say. But good brother I had a long day. I'm fucking these bitches." Leak said laughing. Leaning in, Leak quietly said,

"You heard what happen right?" "Hell, yeah it's a rap for them niggas. When we go outside we can discuss it more, you feel me. Bro, you know how we do." Mizz said reminding Leak of protocol.

They say I couldn't play football, I was too small.
They say I couldn't play basketball, I wasn't tall,
They say I couldn't bag chicks at all.
Now Every Day of My Life I Ball!

"Absolutely cuzin." Leak walked over to a couple of the girls, put his arm around them, and led them to his office. Mizz looked around and saw everyone enjoying themselves and sharing their joy and their accomplishments. He felt good. Thanks to Razah and him, his fam would get to enjoy the finer things. Well at least some of them, he thought looking over and seeing Leak smacking the ass of one of the strippers.

At the convention, even though a whole week has already passed, it was more of the same for Mizz, posing for pictures, signing autographs, and answering questions. He still wasn't completely used to the fame, but he liked it. He looked around trying to find Michaela. Out of the corner of his eye he saw her walking wit her girl, Tess. She was dressed to impress. Wearing nothing but top label designers, she looked like she had just stepped out of a magazine. Not wanting to miss his opportunity, he maneuvered his way through the crowds and headed over to them.

"Hey boy, Mr. Superstar. Shit can't nobody get close to the nigga." Tess both said laughing.

"Girl you ain't lying. He definitely feeling himself. He forgetting the little people. You know how stars do." Michaela laughed.

"You both need to stop," Mizz said jokingly. "Damn you would think we was at a model shoot how fine you both look. Damn, I'm not even going to ask how you been. I see shit." "Boy you crazy, thanks for hooking me up wit a drug dealer! Nice Mizz, real nice. Old Stanky Breath," she laughed, "that corny ass nigga drug dealer. But anyway congrats on the chip, baby."

Mizz laughed. "Thanks girlfriend. I didn't know he

They say I couldn't play football, I was too small.
They say I couldn't play basketball, I wasn't tall,
They say I couldn't bag chicks at all.
Now Every Day of My Life I Ball!

was a dealer. My bad, but I also didn't know he had a dookie mouth either," he said laughing "and Michaela you know you need to stop girl. You know you my heart, so chill out wit the bullshit unless there is something that I don't know." Mizz knew something was up, just not what.

"I'm just joking but after the conference we need to talk seriously." She said looking into his eyes.

"Of course baby, we can definitely do that."

"Shit, I still can't believe Petey, though." Tess said changing the subject.

"I know right, damn it's a shame how you think you know people and you really don't, especially when they try to get into your circle.

"But, I have a question, how you know he was a bitch ass nigga though?" Michaela asked.

"Babe, I'm a street nigga, real recognize real and he was far from both, you dig."

"I give you your props on that for real Mizz," Tess said. "You called him out from the start cuz he sure was a fuk nigga, he was mad corny and he wanted to be thorough wit his hallway piss mouth. Anyways where is your boy Mizz, chocolate nigga?"

"Word! That is definitely new news. Tess, real talk he fukin love you but you ain't heard it from me. I will set that shit up asap, feel me?"

Michaela laughed. "You two are so funny. I'm about to speak. Bitch, I will holla at you later and Mizz I will be looking for you afterwards.

"Ok, I be here waiting on you. Good luck, sexy girl."

"Thanks babe." She walked away thinking to herself how Mizz was being extra nice. She hoped he would be the same way when she told him what was poppin and didn't

They say I couldn't play football, I was too small.
They say I couldn't play basketball, I wasn't tall,
They say I couldn't bag chicks at all.
Now Every Day of My Life I Ball!

act up. She knew how his nigga ass could be. She reached the stage and got a warm welcome from the audience.

Razah walked in just as she started to speak and sat down next to Mizz. "What up sonn, your wifey look dumb good today sonn, word."

"She does, right sonn. Razahhhhhh! Why you late kid?"

"Sonn, I was wit shorty from the party kid she is crazy sonn, word! She got me open b. I think I'm in love."

"Sonn, Razah. B you sound mad nutty right now cuz. You nut ass nigga. Well I'm about to tell you something and you going to forget all about that bird bitch dooke. Why Tess told me you mad sexy and chocolate sonn, word."

"Ewhhhhhhhhhhhhhh cuzin Word!!! sonn you know I love that bitch. I want to get at that b, word forever. Fuk that party stripper bitch."

"Word sonn, you ain't in love no more cuz? Nutty nigga," Mizz laughed. "Sonn, true story. I can't believe she waited so long to say something doggy. Anyway take it to the limit cuzo, word.

"Sonn, she wifey material. Shit, pops own 7 eleven and shit crazy chips and dip b word." Razah said.

"Sonn, you mad funny. But for real, why Michaela telling me that we need to talk, sonn. I think she wanna quit me b. Real talk."

"You mad corny! She love you boy, she just didn't see you in a minute and she misses you a lot and just wanna catch up and talk. Don't worry about it. You straight homie, you good!!! Trust me dooke!" Razah said trying to ease his worries.

"I hope so sonn, hold up you right though sonn, you

They say I couldn't play football, I was too small.
They say I couldn't play basketball, I wasn't tall,
They say I couldn't bag chicks at all.
Now Every Day of My Life I Ball!

right. Here she goes she bout to speak!" Michaela stepped up to the microphone and did a quick little sound check before she began.

"Good evening everyone. First and foremost I wanna thank God, the Almighty for waking me up today. Then, I wanna give a shout out to our president Mizzier for winning the most valuable player of the championship game and winning the first state championship in their school's history. Also our president was voted the number one high school player in the world. Let's give a big round of applause for our president Mizzier Sanders. Mizz, can you come up and say a few words please?"

The crowd roared as Mizz made his way up to the stage.

"Michaela, thanks for that wonderful introduction; it swept me off my feet. I wanna thank God first of all for giving me the strength and opportunity to make all this possible. I wanna thank you, the fans for your support and making it possible for me to shine. I don't want to take any more time from the lovely and beautiful Ms. Michaela, but again thank you and I look forward to seeing you all in the future."

Michaela stepped back up to the podium. "Thank you. Mizz and good luck."

She started her speech and it was well received by the crowd. She talked about goals, and how to achieve them. She also spoke about the convention and the end of the school year and how important it was to stay in school. As she finished she noticed Mizz heading outside. She wasted no time and went after him.

She ran up to him. "Hey boy, you trying to sneak outta here wit out talking to me."

"Of course not baby, it was hot as hell in there. Damn

They say I couldn't play football, I was too small.
They say I couldn't play basketball, I wasn't tall,
They say I couldn't bag chicks at all.
Now Every Day of My Life I Ball!

girl you did work on that speech and had my mind in a different place. Seriously, girl you made me proud to even know who you were. True story."

She blushed slightly. "Thanks, all I do is try to touch people hearts and minds and make them think."

"Since you're into touching people hearts and making them think, let me express something to you. Look, I know shit hasn't been copacetic lately. We had a lot of ups and downs that we both contributed to. Please forgive me for my ignorance and my bullshit and whatever else I've done to make you not feel at ease."

She laughed. "Wow, it's funny what you can say in a room full of hundreds of people that you can't say in front of one person. Even though we weren't talking I never once stopped thinking of you.

"Michaela, you're my heart. I want us t be close again or at least try." Mizz stepped a little closer.

"Really, your timing is always impeccable. You're Mizz the number one everything. You get what you want when and where you want it. Nothing is difficult for you."

"Well, if getting you back isn't mission impossible, difficult is a walk in the park for me. I love you and there is nothing difficult about that."

"Nigga, you always had game I'm just not big on words these days!"

"Ok, ok, I apologized once, but, seriously, I know I fucked up."

"Muthafucker you damn right you fucked up and hurt me, playing me and shit and not taking my feelings into consideration.

"I'm dead ass serious. I miss you, Michaela, and I never miss anyone before in my life and I miss you. I'm in

They say I couldn't play football, I was too small.
They say I couldn't play basketball, I wasn't tall,
They say I couldn't bag chicks at all.
Now Every Day of My Life I Ball!

love wit you."

"Let me tell you something Mr. Mizz this isn't about your black ass this time .Its not about your love Mr. Mizz. It about you can't love me the way I deserve to be loved, that is what this is about." She said trying to fight back the tears that were starting to build behind her eyes.

"You think I'm just saying this shit now! To get cool points, I got nothing better to do but express myself to you." Mizz couldn't understand where he was going wrong.

"Ain't nobody say shit about no cool points, making it about you again. Why you acting like this?" Mizz asked genuinely confused about her reaction.

"What Mizz! Acting like what?" She snapped back.

"Being all ghetto high post and shit. Acting like you don't know me."

"I just finally realized Michaela has to lookout for Michaela cuz no one will lookout for her except her. So I gotta do me and you, Mr. Mizz superstar, gotta do him. In other words I have to take care of my business and I suggest you take care of yours."

"Look Michaela, I know you feeling yourself right know with a lot of scholarship offers and shit and a lot of people wanting you to speak at their functions. You have amazing opportunities opening up for you and shit. But, you and I had fun together, we had a great life. We were friends and companions as well as lovers."

"Ok, Mizz, I can't argue wit you. You're absolutely right. But, give me one reason why I should take you back, one reason. One," she replied, pointing her finger to emphasize the 'one'. She couldn't wait to hear his answer. He stood there silent.

"I thought so. You a sorry muthafucker you know

They say I couldn't play football, I was too small.
They say I couldn't play basketball, I wasn't tall,
They say I couldn't bag chicks at all.
Now Every Day of My Life I Ball!

that. You just as bad as that bitch ass nigga Petey leading people on to think it all good and to find out you ain't shit. Sorry to bust your bubble but I'm pregnant. Now I gotta get all nasty and ghetto so you either going to stand up or be a dead beat dad like the rest of these niggas around your hood cuz I'm having this baby. Either you going to be a part of your baby's life or not." She couldn't hold back the tears anymore. This isn't how she had wanted it to go.

"You what!" Mizz wasn't sure he heard right.

"You heard me nigga, I'm pregnant. So either you gonna stand up or you're not."

"Are you serious? Why didn't you say that shit before?" Now everything made sense.

"Remember when you were being a dick, and I wanted to talk to you and you wouldn't pay me any mind? I wanted to tell you then. But, it didn't happen so I wanted to tell you face to face. I'm sorry but it is what it is and something like this needed to be discussed face to face."

"I'm sorry, you're right and I understand. Of course I laid down and that is my responsibility. I will take care of my seed wit great respect, I love you Michaela and I will be the best father I can be. So how you feel about that?" Michaela's tone changed, softened slightly. "Well if it's a girl we going to name her Meka. It's not a boy so I didn't think of anything," she said laughing. "But, real talk what are we going to do financially? I don't wanna struggle. I don't want our baby in that situation. I wanna know where the baby's next meal is coming from."

"I understand but trust me money is not a problem. We are straight for life, trust me for life. Just don't ask questions." He said putting his arms around her and pulling her close.

They say I couldn't play football, I was too small.
They say I couldn't play basketball, I wasn't tall,
They say I couldn't bag chicks at all.
Now Every Day of My Life I Ball!

"Ok, I trust you."

"One question. Do you love me?" he asked looking down into her eyes.

"I'm scared. Don't hurt me again!"

"Michaela! You're my life now, you and my baby. This baby will have everything I never had and the most important thing our baby will have is love from both parents. This is not a game. Like you told me before there is no "I" in team and we are a team. We are in this matter together and forever. I love you girl. You're now the mother of my child. This is the best gift you can ever give me. I love you." He kissed her gently on her forehead.

"But, I wanna know one question though. If we don't work out, will you turn your back on your kid? And leave her out to dry and be a dead beat and just pay child support. This I need to know so I can be prepared for everything, especially the worst."

"Of course I will always have the best interest of my kid, no matter what happens between you and me."

"Ok. And to answer your question I do love you. Let's make this work again but even better." She leaned in and kissed him. Things were better now. She wasn't going to face this alone. She had a superstar by her side to take care of her. She headed inside to mingle and Mizz went off to find Razah. He found him chatting it up with Tess. "We need to talk, now," he said pulling Razah outside.

"Nigga, this better be good. I was on some ass dude." Razah laughed.

"Nigga, don't worry it is. Yo, b you a godfather nigga. Why Michaela just told me she pregnant."

"Wow! sonn say word b."

"Sonn, word. She knocked up homie. You my man

They say I couldn't play football, I was too small.
They say I couldn't play basketball, I wasn't tall,
They say I couldn't bag chicks at all.
Now Every Day of My Life I Ball!

sonn, so you know what that means, kid."

"What does it mean cuz?" Razah wasn't sure what Mizz was trying to say.

"I'm not in the game b. I'm done. Remember what we talked about sonn. Call an emergency meeting tonight. Sonn, I'm good, we good. Remember what I told you. You going to know when it's time to stop. Sonn between me and you, not counting the candy money, we have 10 million between us and wit the candy money we have over 300 million between us and that's in a year's time. We built an empire. It's not going to last, nothing like that ever lasts, but we don't have to be stupid. I'm done. We on top and no one has a clue, so we need to stop while we are ahead. We will never spend this money in our life time, so we don't need more of it. Let's do something positive wit it now. Real talk." Mizz hoped Razah was on the same page.

"Ok sonn," Razah said nodding his head.

Three hours later everyone sat at the meeting wondering what was going on. Seeing them wearing top of the line designer clothes, diamond rings and custom made shoes, Mizz looked around breathing it all in before getting up to speak. He and Razah had done this. They had given these one time two bit hustlers a taste of the good life. He hoped that after tonight's meeting they wouldn't go back to their old ways but would take the money they had made and make something of themselves and their families. Taking a deep breath he stood up.

"First of all thanks fam for all of you coming out tonight on such late notice. I know some of you niggas got kids and shit and it's late. I love each and every one of you and we made a lot of money because of one thing, loyalty. But unfortunately it's a wrap. It's all over." The words

They say I couldn't play football, I was too small.
They say I couldn't play basketball, I wasn't tall,
They say I couldn't bag chicks at all.
Now Every Day of My Life I Ball!

hung in the air as everyone looked at one another, confused.

"What the fuck you talking 'bout Mizz? That Petey shit was some bullshit. Don't sweat that. We good. Let's get that money."

"Nah, I'm serious fam it's over I'm done and out. Look, all of you in this room is a millionaire at least ten times over each one of one. Petey was awake up call. If you nigga keep up the bullshit you will get caught and I don't wanna see it. As for me, my girl just told me she's pregnant and that's another wake up call for me. I wanna see my kid grow up and not have me locked up for some bullshit or capped cuz niggas is jealous. We all have millions and millions more than we can ever spend in our lifetime, that's real talk. We had a hell of a run, no jail time no one dead. We hustled right. There is no need to go wrong now. There is no need to be greedy, but do what you want. I can't tell you what to do but I don't have to be a part of it. But for me, it starts now and I have to wash this money right and do something constructive wit that money, like build a future for my family, give my kid the life growing up I didn't have. I can't do that if I'm dead or behind bars. I need to be that positive role model for my kid. I just don't wanna be known as Mizz the ball player. I wanna be known to my kid's dad, and be the best father a kid can have. I wanna be Mizz the hero, man, not Mizz the hustler. Don't want them to say, "He was a great b ball player but he's a loser in jail." That's not me, fam. I hustled to get ahead not to make a life outta it or a living. I was able and fortunate to make my life decision, my destiny. I want my kid to be able to make theirs. And right now," Mizz turned to Razah in agreement, "it's time for you to make yours."

They say I couldn't play football, I was too small.
They say I couldn't play basketball, I wasn't tall,
They say I couldn't bag chicks at all.
Now Every Day of My Life I Ball!

Epilogue

In the early morning hours, Mizz and Razah stood shoulder to shoulder watching in New York silence as the sun snuck up slowly on their city. The iconic skyline was flooded in streaming golden light as a curtain of haze draped itself against the clouds and skyscrapers as the sun's beams played along the sidewalk under the boy's feet. Anyone rushing by them would see two seemingly casual observers in the game of life, when in actuality; no two men were ever more serious players than these. While each was lost in his own thoughts, tight as they were, and would prove to be for life, they confidently starred down the future together without so much as blinking. Between them they held one singular and binding thought: today, yes, they felt quite certain that today the sun, the city, and life itself, was shining on them, just for them, and it felt good.

The End

They say I couldn't play football, I was too small.
They say I couldn't play basketball, I wasn't tall,
They say I couldn't bag chicks at all.
Now Every Day of My Life I Ball!

Author's Note

What has this story taught us especially in the time and age and era that we live in? It's shown us that life is continuous. Its ignorance and intelligence, tragedy, deception, self empowerment and self destruction; the good times and the bad times. But what it all boils down to is what life decisions you make and what paths you take. In this game of life, nine outta ten times people choose greed which then brings death and deception. In the blink of an eye you can go from rags to riches. Loyalty and respect are the real keys to success. Its not money, power and respect. That ends up in even more money but also more problems. In the end, you control your own destiny. It's not your environment that controls the outcome of your life. No matter what you do or say, you still have to look yourself in the mirror and face yourself, and your decisions.

They say in this game that this is the life that you chose, no matter how long you been hustling, 5-10-15-20 years scrapping, struggling, scheming, lying, cheating, stealing, fucking, pimping, manipulating, begging, and shiestyness. When your run is done, what's left? Imprisonment? Death? Then what? A hole in the ground? You can't take nothing wit you when you go. No cars, jewelry, money, nothing when you six feet deep. Be real with yourself. Don't be a product of your environment. Be a product of your imagination.

They say I couldn't play football, I was too small.
They say I couldn't play basketball, I wasn't tall,
They say I couldn't bag chicks at all.
Now Every Day of My Life I Ball!